Murder in Lancashire

A Samantha Degan Mystery
by
Jane O'Brien

For information, email **Cozy Cat Press**, cozycatpress@aol.com or visit our website at: www.cozycatpress.com

COZY CAT
P R E S S

ISBN: 978-1-946063-17-5

Printed in the United States of America

Cover design by Paula Ellenberger
www.paulaellenberger.com

1 2 3 4 5 6 7 8 9 10

A heartfelt thank you to my family, friends and readers who have encouraged me to continue my writing.

PROLOGUE

"Are you sure you want to go to this thing tonight?" Detective Joseph Fletcher asked Samantha Degan as he nibbled her neck.

"I want to go, but if you keep doing that, I might very well change my mind."

Detective Fletcher, otherwise known as Fletch, was a confirmed bachelor until he'd met Samantha. Their meeting was somewhat unorthodox as he was arresting her for murder at the time. Happily, her innocence was proven and the real culprit was brought to justice.

Samantha was a writer whose first non-fiction work, *Memoirs of Professor Fenwick Stonehill*, had recently been published. Professor Stonehill had been the victim of a brutal murder before the completion of his autobiography. Samantha had received local notoriety as the author of the book and had come to the attention of the mayor of Lancaster, Richard Delaney. The mayor was young, good-looking, and had a propensity for attracting beautiful women.

"I could always call Robin; she likes musicals and Frank won't mind going with her," said Samantha.

"Don't you think Frank would complain about seeing some lame musical?" Fletch asked.

"Have you ever seen *The Music Man*? It was a movie several years ago and it's really quite wonderful with a lot of good music."

"I've told you about Mayor Delaney's reputation with the ladies," said Fletch, "The only reason he asked me to go to this thing is because he wanted to see you again."

"Detective Fletcher, are you jealous?"

"I would be if I thought you were attracted to him, but I know you're a one-woman guy and I'm that guy," he said, smiling at her.

"Aren't we sure of ourselves?" she replied, knowing it was the truth.

*****

The Lancashire Community Theater had ample seating for large audiences. It was used for everything from political rallies to high school graduations. The Lancashire Community Players were considered one of the top amateur performing companies in the state.

The lobby was bustling with patrons when Samantha and Fletch arrived. Mayor Delaney spotted them immediately and pushed his way through the crowd.

"I'm glad you two could make it tonight," he said and handed each of them a ticket. "You'll sit with my group in the center section."

The doors opened and the crowd began to filter into the auditorium.

"How much do you want to bet you're seated next to His Honor?" whispered Fletch.

"Don't be silly; he handed us these tickets randomly. Did you get a look at the blonde on his arm? I don't think you have to worry that he'll be lusting after me tonight."

Fletch gave her a sly smile when they reached their row. Richard Delaney patted the space next to him, indicating Samantha's seat.

The mayor was on his best behavior during the first act of the musical. However, Samantha noticed that he began inching toward her during the second act. Moving to her right as much as possible didn't seem to discourage him.

Finally, the last scene was being played out on stage. It was difficult not to tap one's toe to the music of *Seventy-Six Trombones*. The cast, including Sophia Delaney, the mayor's wife as Marian, the librarian, walked off the apron of the stage and up the two center aisles of the theater, playing instruments or singing while the orchestra performed the lively tune. The audience clapped and shouted their approval until the noise level was deafening. Suddenly, Samantha felt the mayor's head on her shoulder. Her body stiffened when he slumped onto her lap.

She was frozen in her seat as the audience stood to applaud the fine performance. Fletch saw the look of horror on Samantha's face, he reached over and lifted the mayor's head off her lap. Quickly dialing 911 on his cell phone with one hand, he settled Richard Delaney's lifeless body back into his theater seat. The blonde to the injured man's right was oblivious to what was happening right next to her. Turning to say something to Richard, she saw his dead body and let out a blood-curdling scream which was drowned out by the music and the noise of the crowded theater.

Eventually, people seated around the mayor began to back away as they saw blood oozing from his head. Samantha regained her composure as best she could, and stood over Mayor Richard Delaney as Fletch administered CPR.

CHAPTER 1

The actors circled around the theater and marched to the stage when the curtains opened again. The applause was deafening, Sophia Delaney glanced toward Richard's reserved seat. She could see that something was terribly wrong, and she ran off the front edge of the stage and down to her husband.

"Richard!" she called out as she ran up the aisle to where his body lay. Bending next to him, she quickly realized he was bleeding and barely breathing, "Richard, don't leave me; I need you," she sobbed.

Samantha put her arm around the woman's shoulder and urged her to move away when the paramedics came rushing down the aisle. Richard was lifted onto a stretcher and rushed out of the theater to the waiting ambulance. Sophia followed, leaving the blonde behind to fend for herself.

"He was shot in the head," Fletch whispered in Samantha's ear. "Whoever fired the weapon must have walked up the side aisle on the left. I'll check around to ask if anyone saw anything suspicious. Will you be all right staying here with the blonde?"

"I'll be fine. Do what you need to do."

Samantha turned toward the girl who was still visibly upset.

"I'm Samantha Degan; what's your name?"

"Megan, Megan Fairbanks. Is the mayor going to be all right?"

"I don't know, Megan. Are you and Mayor Delaney close friends?" she asked, not meaning to pry.

"No, I just started working in his office. I'm a receptionist at the front desk. My boyfriend wasn't happy when I told him I'd be coming here with my boss. He's heard stories that Mayor Delaney is a lecher and I couldn't make him understand that it's part of my job. You don't think Jimmy tried to kill him, do you?"

"I don't know, Megan; do you think it's possible? Does Jimmy own a gun?"

"He has a gun he uses for hunting. I hate the thing and make him keep it locked in his truck. He was mad tonight, but I don't think he'd kill anybody."

"I doubt the weapon that injured the mayor was a hunting rifle. Why don't you call Jimmy to tell him what happened; you don't want him to worry about your safety if he hears about this on the news."

"Jimmy never watches the news, but I'll call him."

Samantha listened to Megan's side of the conversation.

"Hi, Jimmy. What are you doing? No, I'm fine. Are you home? Can you come to the theater to pick me up? No, the mayor can't take me home because he's in the hospital. Somebody shot him. Oh, Jimmy, it was terrible! He had blood coming out of his mouth. Okay, I'll wait for you out front. Yes, you were right; I should have stayed home with you."

"Is Jimmy home?" asked Samantha.

"Yes, and he's really mad at me now."

"Megan, I heard you say you'd meet him out front. I think Detective Fletcher will want to ask you some questions first. Maybe you should call him back and tell him to wait until you're able to leave."

"Jimmy won't like that."

Samantha told herself that the way this girl's boyfriend treated her was none of her concern.

Fletch joined Samantha again.

"Nobody saw anything unusual; they were watching the center aisles when the shooting took place. Whoever was responsible for this was able to get away unnoticed."

"Fletch, this is Megan Fairbanks; the mayor invited her as his guest this evening. Her boyfriend will be picking her up shortly."

"Hello, Megan; can you tell me what you saw and heard tonight?"

"I didn't see anything. I was watching the show. Wasn't it a wonderful? The only other time I've ever seen anything like it was in high school and this was so much better. When I turned to thank Mayor Delaney for inviting me, all I saw was blood. I think I screamed, but I don't remember."

"Do you know Mayor Delaney well?"

"I don't know him at all. His executive assistant, Cindy, told me he wanted me to come with him tonight. Like I told Samantha, my boyfriend didn't like it one bit. The mayor's driver picked me up at home. It was only the second time I'd ever seen the mayor. He was very nice on the ride here and talked about the show and how his wife was starring in it."

"I'd like to talk with your boyfriend; would you call him and ask him to come into the theater? I'll alert the police officer at the door to let him in."

"I'll tell him but he won't like it; he doesn't like cops."

"Not everyone does, but I'd like to ask him a few questions."

*****

Twenty minutes later, Jimmy was led to an office next to the lobby where Fletch had interviewed several of the theater goers. He was exactly the way Samantha had pictured him, tall and muscular with tattoos covering his arms. He had a look of defiance when he strutted into the office. He glared at Megan and she gave him a sheepish look.

"What did that guy do to you?" he demanded. "I told you I didn't want you to go out with him and now look at you."

Fletch introduced himself and began his questions.

"You were upset because Megan came to the theater with her boss, is that correct?"

"Yeah, I was pissed. Whoever heard of a boss who demands a stupid girl go out with him at night. What kind of a jerk does he think I am?"

"What did you do while Megan was gone, Jimmy?"

"I didn't do nothing. I watched a flick on TV and drank a beer." He glared at Megan. "You were supposed to buy me a six-pack on the way home from your precious job. I only had one left." He looked at Fletch. "That pissed me off too."

"Did it piss you off enough to come down here to see what Megan and the mayor were up to?"

"No, what are you saying? Are you asking if I came down here to shoot the jerk? I wouldn't shoot him; I'd let these do *my* talking." He held up his clenched fists.

"You can go now. Leave your full name and address with the officer."

Fletch turned to Megan and quietly asked her if she would like someone to take her to a friend or relative's house for the night.

"No, Jimmy won't hurt me; he likes to shoot his mouth off but he's really a good guy."

Samantha had a sickening feeling in her stomach. Megan was a pretty girl who was in an abusive relationship whether she knew it or not.

Fletch's phone rang; he answered and turned to Samantha. "The mayor just died."

CHAPTER 2

Sophia Delaney was still wearing the early nineteen hundred's era costume from the show while nervously pacing in the waiting area of the emergency department of Lancashire Hospital.

"Try not to worry, Mrs. Delaney," said Charles, the mayor's driver. "Mayor Delaney is young and healthy; he'll be just fine."

"I hope you're right, Charles, but you didn't see his face when they wheeled him out of the theater. Somebody shot him in the head. I can't believe that detective was practically sitting next to him and he didn't stop the person who was trying to assassinate my husband."

"The theater was filled with people and nobody knew what was happening. Is there someone I can call for you? Eloise is on her way, but is there someone else you'd like to have with you?"

"No, Charles, there's no one else."

Eloise Kittredge was the mayor's campaign manager. It was well-known in political circles that Richard Delaney's ambitions extended far beyond the office of mayor of Lancashire. He would be announcing his intention to run for governor of the state within the next few months. The governorship was only another stepping stone to his real wish—that of the President of the United States. Eloise and Sophia knew his plan and supported him wholeheartedly.

"Here's Eloise now."

Eloise, an attractive, slightly overweight woman in her late fifties, had developed an interest in politics years ago. She was a shrewd judge of character and had seen something appealing in the twenty-nine-year-old lawyer who had contacted her when someone told him he should run for mayor. What the young fellow lacked in experience and knowledge of governmental workings, he made up for in charisma. He had been married to a local actress and singer for five years. They had no children and neither had any desire to become parents.

Eloise had taken both of them under her wing. She was intrigued, but not surprised at their personal life. Although the pair seemed to love each other, Sophia spent many nights away from home, devoting herself to her craft. Richard appeared at many social and community functions, always with a woman, preferably blonde, by his side. Sophia acknowledged that her husband was an incurable flirt, but she never appeared bothered by it. She was happy to be excused from the public activities her husband enjoyed. Nights spent rehearsing lines or pampering herself in a bubble bath while indulging in a glass of sparkling champagne were more to her liking.

*****

Doctor Eugene Preston, the emergency room physician, who'd cared for Richard, walked out of the treatment area and spotted Sophia. The doctor asked her to come into a private consultation room. Fearing what the doctor was going to say, Sophia grabbed Eloise's hand and held it tightly.

"I'm sorry, Mrs. Delaney; we did everything we could. The damage was extensive and your husband did not survive."

Sophia's knees were weak and she held the doctor's arm, afraid of collapsing on the floor of the hospital.

"May I see him?" she asked.

"Yes, of course. Wait here; the nurse will come to get you."

Sophia regained her composure and was determined not to fall apart. The nurse led her to a cubical where she looked in horror at the lifeless body of her husband.

"I'll leave you alone, Mrs. Delaney."

Sophia took Richard's hand in hers and wept quietly. Eloise placed her strong hand on her friend's shoulder.

"It's time to let him go, Sophia," she heard her say.

"I can't do this, Eloise. I can't say goodbye to Richard."

"You're a strong woman, Sophia—stronger than you think. Charles will drive you home and I'll follow in my car. You need to get some rest tonight. I'll stay with you. Tomorrow we'll make funeral arrangements."

They walked to the lobby together. Fletch and Samantha were waiting for them.

"Mrs. Delaney, I'm very sorry for your loss. I'd like to ask you some questions if you're up to it."

"Can it wait until tomorrow, Detective? Mrs. Delaney is understandably distraught this evening."

"Yes, of course. I'll call in the morning to arrange a convenient time."

*****

Fletch waited for the doctor to finish his report. The bullet had been recovered from the mayor's brain and was being transported to the forensic laboratory for examination, and comparison if the murder weapon was ever recovered.

Reporters began to converge in the hospital waiting room.

"Is it true, Detective Fletcher, you were sitting next to the mayor when he was shot?"

"Did you see the shooter, Detective Fletcher?"

"How well did you know the mayor, Ms. Degan?"

"Were you Mayor Delaney's latest paramour, Ms. Degan?"

Samantha glared at the reporters.

"I met Mayor Delaney for the first time two nights ago. He was kind enough to offer me two tickets to the performance this evening. We were nothing more than acquaintances."

"Fellas, the investigation of Mayor Delaney's death is in the beginning stages. Chief Williams will answer any questions."

Fletch took Samantha's arm and disappeared into a private office where Doctor Preston was waiting to answer Fletch's medical questions.

The reporters and photographers paced the room waiting for the transfer of the body to the hospital morgue.

After giving his statement, Doctor Preston pointed to a seldom used doorway where the couple escaped to the parking lot and away from the prying reporters.

"Do I look like a loose woman?" asked Samantha when they were safely on their way. "Those reporters thought I was Mayor Delaney's lover. You thought I was the professor's lover when he was killed. Maybe I'd better start wearing my hair in a bun at the back of my neck and tone down the makeup."

"Don't you dare change anything; you're perfect the way you are. Besides, I never really thought you were the professor's lover."

"No, you just thought I was his murderer."

Fletch looked sheepishly at Samantha and decided to change the subject.

"I'm going to stay with you tonight in case one of the more aggressive reporters stakes out your apartment."

"I'd like that but I don't think it's necessary. I told them I barely knew the mayor."

"Some of those guys are just waiting to report anything they think might be scandalous. Mayor Delaney had a reputation with beautiful young women."

"That reminds me, I hope Megan Fairbanks is all right. I'm worried about that boyfriend of hers. She gave me her phone number. I'll give her a call in the morning."

"Yeah, I had him spotted for a bully when he swaggered through the theater doors. She wouldn't be the first nice girl to become involved with his type."

*****

For the first time since they'd become a couple, Megan Fairbanks was afraid of Jimmy. She couldn't make him understand that the evening with her boss was all business.

"Jimmy, I swear Mayor Delaney didn't put a move on me. He was a total gentleman. I was just doing my job. I didn't want to go to that musical tonight any more than you wanted me to."

"Did you like being there."

"Oh yes, Jimmy. I've never seen anything like it; it was a fantastic story and the music was beautiful. I had a terrific time."

"I knew it," he said as he raised his fist toward her but stopped himself.

Megan had told Samantha Degan that Jimmy wouldn't hurt her, but now she wasn't so sure. Maybe he'd followed her. He said he only had one beer. Was that because he was in the theater instead of at home? Detective Fletcher said there was a side entrance where the killer could have entered. Jimmy could open a locked door; he'd done it in the past, but his criminal days were over. Was Jimmy capable of committing murder? Was she in love with a killer? Were her feelings love or the need to reform him?

CHAPTER 3

"When are you going to break down and marry me?" Fletch asked while he and Samantha were eating breakfast the next morning.

"We've only known each other a matter of months. Marriage is a lifetime commitment; we have to be sure it's what we really want," answered Samantha.

"I'm sure I love you and always will, Samantha. I spend more nights here than I do in my own apartment Think of all the money we'd save on rent if we were married."

Samantha didn't have any doubt she and Fletch were meant to be together; she wanted to enjoy the courtship part of their relationship. Between her studies and part-time jobs, there hadn't been time for a social life while she attended the university.

"Let's talk about this tonight. You have a crime to solve and I need to get to work. I've neglected my writing lately and have thought about hiring an assistant."

"Wonderful idea, then you'll have more time to spend with me," Fletch said, as he nuzzled her neck.

"I can't think when you do that, Detective."

"Good. For what I have in mind, thinking isn't required."

"Hold that thought. Now, get out of here before I get further behind than I already am."

Reluctantly, he kissed her goodbye and was out the door.

Samantha poured herself another cup of coffee and sat down at her desk in the living room. *This place is too small for two people. It would be nice to have a bigger apartment and my own office. Even better would be a little house with a white picket fence. Maybe not too little; we'll need the room when the babies start coming along. Maybe it's time to start planning a wedding. I don't want Fletch to get tired of waiting while I make up my mind.*

The stack of correspondence and invitations to speak at various functions was growing taller; the memoirs of her former employer had brought notoriety that she never expected. Professor Stonehill was a well-known figure at the university as well as the community of Lancashire. In the short time Samantha had worked for him, she had listened to and loved his storytelling. She learned more about the man in the few short months before his death than most people know about another person in a lifetime.

He was a fascinating and well-loved figure. It was a surprise to Samantha that his stories were so easy to tell and were received so well by an audience.

The note with Megan Fairbanks's phone number was lying on her desk. She looked for a reason to call the girl because of her concern about the boyfriend's obvious anger. As Megan was a receptionist at Mayor Delaney's office and might now be out of a job, Samantha realized she had the perfect excuse to call her. She would offer her a job as her assistant and free up time for Samantha to do what she loved—writing her mysteries.

*****

Megan arrived at the mayor's office on time, although she hadn't had much sleep the night before. Cindy Matthews, the mayor's executive assistant, greeted Megan with tears streaming down her cheeks.

"Megan, you were there when it happened, I can't believe the mayor is gone. It must have been horrible for you. You didn't have to come to work today, but I'm glad you did. The phones haven't stopped ringing and the reporters are swarming in the lobby. Do you think you're up to facing them this morning?"

"I think so. I'm sure they won't recognize me as the one sitting next to Mayor Delaney when it happened. They didn't know I was there."

Megan walked through the inner office door to the reception area.

"It's her!" shouted one reporter

They bombarded her with questions:

"How long were you having an affair with the mayor?"

"Were you and Samantha Degan rivals for the mayor's attention?"

"Does Mrs. Delaney know about your relationship with her husband?"

Megan stood motionless, unable to move, the questions so stunned her. Andy, the security guard, did his best to move the reporters and photographers back but there were too many for the slight young man to control.

Cindy heard the commotion and stepped to the front lobby, pulling Megan back into the office. She closed the door behind them.

Detective Fletcher and his partner, Robin Wells, walked into the building.

"Fellas, go easy on the girl, she's an innocent bystander in this."

"Fletch, did you see this picture in *The Globe* this morning? It looks like she was hardly innocent where Mayor Delaney was concerned."

Fletch looked at the newspaper and saw a picture of the mayor with his arm around Megan Fairbanks.

Megan was smiling and the mayor looked at her in adoration.

"Fellas, you know the mayor liked to have young women around him. This girl is an employee who was doing her job last night. There's nothing in this photo that indicates a relationship between the two of them."

"Why are you here, Fletch? Who do you and Robin suspect of murder?"

"Robin and I are conducting routine interviews with anyone who knew Mayor Delaney. We will report our findings to Chief Williams. He's scheduled a news conference for two o'clock this afternoon. At that time, you'll be informed of any developments we're able to divulge in the case."

"We're waiting to interview Mayor Delaney's replacement, Forrest Wakefield. Is he a suspect?"

"Let us get through and I'll see what I can find out. I know you fellas are just doing your job but so am I, and that means keeping some order here."

*****

The reporters let Fletch and Robin pass. Andy unlocked the door for them and they walked into the office.

Megan was crying. It was obvious the events of the previous night and this morning had caught up with her. Cindy had her arm around the girl trying to calm her.

"Jimmy will be furious when he sees that," she said, looking at the picture published on the front page of *The Globe.*

"Hello, Megan."

"Hello, Detective Fletcher; are you here to question me again?"

"Not only you, Megan, we're here to question everyone."

He introduced himself and Detective Wells to Cindy. "What can I do to help?" Cindy asked.

"The biggest help now is for the acting mayor to talk to the reporters out there. Is Mr. Wakefield here?"

"He's here. He's having his hair styled now to make himself look younger for the cameras." Cindy couldn't hold back a slight chuckle.

"Maybe he won't mind talking to us while he's being styled," said Robin. "We won't be taking any pictures."

Cindy walked with them down the hallway to the office of the acting mayor.

"He's made himself comfortable," Fletch whispered to Robin.

"Acting Mayor Wakefield, I'm sorry to interrupt. May I introduce you to Detective Fletcher and Detective Wells? They're here to ask you some questions and they promise not to take any photographs."

Forrest Wakefield was a short, pudgy sixty-three-year-old man. His thick gray hair was his best feature. He glanced at the detectives and smiled.

"I hope you don't think I'm vain, but I do want to look good in the newspapers. Richard was very photogenic without even trying. I'm afraid I must put a little more effort into looking presentable.

"I'm sure you're going to ask me where I was last evening when Mayor Delaney was so viciously gunned down. It was my wife's birthday and we were out to dinner with friends. We were at Chung Lee's Chinese restaurant from seven-thirty until after ten o'clock."

"I'm surprised you weren't at the theater last night for Mrs. Delaney's performance," said Robin.

"Oh, my dear, you don't understand. My dear wife, Margaret, and Sophia Delaney do not get along. I have managed to stay married for thirty-five years because I don't ask my bride to do anything she doesn't want to do. Spending her birthday watching that woman on stage, would definitely not be something she would want to do."

"What were your feelings toward Mayor Delaney?" Fletch asked.

"Let me just say, he had the looks to be mayor, but I have the brains. I'm sorry the lad is dead, but I'm happy to represent our fair city as it should be represented. Now, please excuse me; I have a press conference to give—my first as acting mayor." He put on his somber face to meet the reporters.

Wanda Anderson, Forrest's assistant, watched smiling when her boss walked out of his office and through the doors to the conference room where the reporters were waiting for him to speak.

"Ms. Anderson," said Robin, "Detective Fletcher and I would like to ask you some questions about Mayor Delaney."

"Of course, I'll be happy to answer any questions you might have. I must admit, I believe Richard Delaney was overrated; Forrest Wakefield was the true mayor of Lancashire and now he'll get the credit he deserves."

"How long have you worked for Mr. Wakefield?"

"I began working for Forrest twenty-two years ago. He had an accounting firm in town. He had a staff of ten people and I was the office manager. I met Eloise Kittredge at a political rally; Richard hired her as his campaign manager five years ago. She's the one who put the idea into my head that Forrest would be a good fit as deputy mayor. Forrest was reluctant to leave the accounting firm in the hands of his brother-in-law, but the more he thought about it, the more interested he became. Eloise and I set up a meeting with Forrest and Richard. Richard could see immediately that Forrest was the man who would make him look good. They came to an agreement that very day.

"It was a good relationship until about six months ago when Richard's real ambition became clear. He planned to run for governor and eventually, president of the United States. Forrest was certain he'd be asked to follow him as the next lieutenant governor, but Richard had other ideas. He told Forrest he wanted a young administration and Forrest wouldn't fit in with his plans.

"I knew Forrest was crushed, although he hid his disappointment well. He had come to love government work and now he was being cast aside because of his age."

"Mr. Wakefield must have been angry with the mayor," said Fletch.

"He was more hurt than angry. The sad thing is, Richard would have easily won the election for governor, but without Forrest guiding him, his governorship would have been a disaster for our state."

"You don't have a very high opinion of Richard Delaney."

"No, I don't. Look around you, Detective. Excluding me and the few men in these offices, all you see are pretty, young women. Richard was always seen with one of the staff dangling from his arm. It was shameful. His wife never accompanied him to social functions and didn't seem to mind that he was flaunting his bevy of blondes, as Forrest called them. The man was a womanizer if you ask me."

"Thank you, Ms. Anderson. If you think of anything else that will be helpful in solving this case, please call me." Fletch handed her his card.

The detectives walked out of the office, and Robin whispered, "I'd say Ms. Wanda Anderson is in love with her boss."

"I'd have to agree; it wouldn't surprise me if Wanda decided to eliminate the ambitious Mayor Delaney herself. It seems to have worked out well for Acting Mayor Wakefield."

"Maybe we should have asked where Ms. Anderson was last night, although she was probably home with her cats."

"How do you know she has cats?"

"Because I know you're allergic to cat hair and your eyes are red and puffy. Didn't you see the cat hair all over her sweater?"

"You do make a good detective, partner," he said as he rubbed his eyes.

"Here, take one of these."

Robin pulled an antihistamine tablet out of her purse.

"Who's going to take care of me when you go on maternity leave?"

"That might be sooner than I thought; this pregnancy hasn't been as easy as the first two."

"This one must be a girl; girls are more difficult than boys."

"Detective Fletcher, you are such a chauvinist. I don't know why Samantha and I put up with you."

"Because I'm loveable. Shall we pay a visit to the widow Delaney?"

CHAPTER 4

On her way home from a breakfast meeting with a woman's group at the Lutheran church, Samantha spotted a copy of *The Globe* outside the drug store. She recognized Megan Fairbanks with Richard Delaney on the cover, looking like a couple. The photograph was very suggestive with Richard's arm around Megan's waist. The first thought in Samantha's mind was that Jimmy would see it and jump to the wrong conclusion.

She had intended to call Megan and hurried home to look for the phone number she'd left on her desk.

*****

"Megan, this is Samantha Degan. We met last night at the theater."

"Hello, Samantha," a voice said tearfully.

"Are you all right, Megan?"

"I'm all right, I think. Oh, Samantha, there was an awful picture of Mayor Delaney and me in the paper this morning. It wasn't like that. I don't remember him putting his arm around me. If Jimmy sees it, he'll be so mad."

"Are you at work now?"

"Yes. Reporters were here earlier and wanted to know if I was the mayor's latest lover. Cindy told me I could go home but I don't know how I would explain my leaving work early to Jimmy."

"Would you like to come to my apartment? We can talk about the newspaper article and figure out how to explain it to Jimmy."

"Are you sure you don't mind? I would really like to get out of here. Everyone is staring at me. I wish I'd never taken this job."

Samantha gave her directions to the apartment building and answered correspondence while waiting for Megan to arrive.

*****

"Megan, it's not the end of the world. Remember, I was sitting on the other side of Mayor Delaney and I know you didn't do anything wrong. If it makes you feel better, the reporters at the hospital last night accused *me* of being the mayor's lover too."

"Well, that's dumb. Why would you be interested in Mayor Delaney when you have that hunk, Detective Fletcher?"

"He is a hunk, isn't he?" Samantha agreed. "Let's talk about you. Is your family in Lancashire?"

"No, I'm from Williamson. Jimmy wanted to move here a couple of months ago. He was tired of the police following him around. He's had problems with the law a few times but he was really trying to stay out of trouble. My parents don't like Jimmy, but I love him and wanted to come with him."

"You must have started working for the mayor's office shortly after you arrived."

"Yes, there aren't too many jobs out there. Cindy, that's the mayor's executive assistant, told me I'd be able to advance quickly, so I accepted the receptionist job. I took business classes in high school and I was going to the community college until I moved here."

"I could use someone with clerical skills, although it would only be part-time."

"Oh, my goodness. I would love to work for you. I had a part-time job at the library in Williamson and read your book when it was first published., I've read it twice, that's how much I liked it."

"If you think thirty hours will be enough, you're hired."

"I'm sure it will be enough. Jimmy likes me to be home early to fix his supper, so he'll be happy about the hours."

"Where does Jimmy work?"

"He works construction when they need him."

Samantha wondered how the young couple paid rent on an apartment and bought groceries with Jimmy only working when he was needed. Construction workers made a decent wage, but if he didn't work, he didn't make any money at all. The term *drug dealer* went through her mind. She'd have to see about getting a background check on Megan. She'd never hired anyone before and didn't think it through before offering the job. She liked Megan, and had good instincts about her. Jimmy was another story.

Samantha's organizational skills made it easy for Megan to catch on to what was expected of her. She loved reading and especially mysteries and was happy to be working with a mystery writer.

*****

Jimmy called on her cell phone, "Where are you? I stopped by the mayor's office and they said you weren't there. Do you have a new boss? Is he dating you too, like the old one?"

"Jimmy, I wasn't on a date with Mayor Delaney. I wish you would believe me. You met my new boss last night, Samantha Degan, the writer. Jimmy, I'm so excited. I think this will be a terrific job."

"I don't like it. You don't have to work at all. Why are you doing this to me?"

"Doing what, Jimmy? I like working. What would I do all day if I stayed home?"

"You could take care of me," he said and then thought better of it. *If she's around all day, she'll get on my nerves. It's best that I'm alone in the mornings.* "Never mind, you can work for Samantha what's her name, but I want you home at night, do you understand?"

"Yes, Jimmy, I understand."

Samantha heard only one side of the conversation but could imagine what was said by Jimmy. She didn't trust that guy and hoped Megan would see him for who he was before it was too late.

CHAPTER 5

Fletch drove to Sophia Delaney's home with Robin directing him. The home backed up to the Lancashire Country Club and was an impressive white two-story home surrounded by trees.

"You should run for mayor, Fletch. Samantha might agree to marry you if you offer her a house like this."

"Do you think that would do it?" he laughed.

Colorful flowers edged the sides of the cobblestone walkway leading to the front door. Fletch pushed the door bell.

Eloise Kittredge greeted them.

"Hello, detectives. Sophia is expecting you."

She led them into a beautifully decorated room with a wall of windows overlooking the golf course.

"You have a lovely home, Mrs. Delaney," said Robin.

"Thank you; this is Richard's dream house, not mine. I'd prefer a small cottage away from the city."

"Mrs. Delaney, are you willing to answer questions this afternoon?"

"Yes, Detective. I'd like to help you find whoever did this to my husband. I know our marriage was unconventional, but I did love him in my way."

"Do you suspect anyone of the crime, ma'am?"

"I have no one in mind. Richard had enemies, mainly husbands or boyfriends of the blondes who always hung on him in public. Richard loved the attention of women. I knew that when I married him and I decided early in our relationship that he was never going to be a one-woman man. I never did like the social life, but I would have accompanied him to any function he attended. However, I cramped his style. I'm not sure why he married me."

"Are you saying you weren't the least bit jealous of the women? I know, if my husband took someone other than me to a party, he'd live to regret it."

"Maybe a little when we were first married, but I was willing to put up with his behavior, especially after he became mayor. You see, I love performing but I'm aware that I'm not great at acting or singing. I'm good, mind you, but without Richard, I wouldn't have gotten as far as I have. My career has advanced since becoming the wife of the mayor. It's the worst kept secret that Richard's ambition meant he would settle for nothing less than the presidency of the United States. If you're thinking I might have arranged to have him killed, I can assure you, a living Richard was more beneficial to me than a dead one."

"Actors are notorious for their inflated egos; you seem to prefer being out of the spotlight."

"You'd be surprised how many of us are introverts. When I'm on stage, I become a different person. I love the glare of the lights and the applause of the audience. You see, I live in two different worlds, and both are delightful in their way."

*****

After a few more questions, the detectives took their leave.

"Sophia is a very interesting woman," said Robin.

"Also, a better actress than she gives herself credit for. I didn't buy all that garbage about accepting her husband's philandering. I can't believe any woman or man, for that matter, would be that tolerant."

"You think the murder was a professional job, don't you, Fletch?"

"Either a professional or an expert marksman. Assuming Richard Delaney was the intended victim, it would take an expert to hit his or her target with one bullet, especially in a crowded theater."

"I'd like to know why Mrs. Wakefield dislikes Sophia Delaney. Do you suppose it's because of Sophia's title of First Lady of Lancashire? It's obvious Mr. Wakefield resented not being mayor while Richard was in office. maybe Mrs. Wakefield felt the same way about being the first lady."

"Samantha has been the guest speaker at the country club on several occasions. I know she doesn't like dealing with Mrs. Wakefield, and Samantha gets along well with everyone. I'll ask her about it tonight."

*****

Samantha was happy with the way Megan took charge in her new job. She was glad she'd hired her, but there was a nagging feeling in the back of her mind that it would have been better to have gone through the proper hiring procedure before giving her a job. Jimmy had too great a hold on her. *Maybe the nagging feeling had more to do with Jimmy than with Megan.*

"Samantha, you have so many requests for speaking engagements, I don't know how you get any writing done."

"It does keep me busy but I'm glad people are still interested in discussing Professor Stonehill. Shouldn't you be heading home? It's almost four o'clock."

"I just want to finish sorting this correspondence for you. I know you like to answer your fan letters yourself. Maybe I can make it easier for you by addressing the envelopes. I'll do that tomorrow if you haven't changed your mind about hiring me."

"Megan, you have only been here a matter of hours and I'm already wondering what I did without you."

Megan smiled and was grateful for the compliment. She liked Samantha and liked working for her. Jimmy would be happy her boss was a woman. She wasn't anxious to go home to Jimmy tonight. He wouldn't hurt her physically. He wasn't always kind with his words but that didn't mean he didn't love her. Last night had been her fault; she shouldn't have gone to the theater with Mayor Delaney. It wasn't a date but Jimmy couldn't be blamed for being angry about it. If she hadn't gone, her picture wouldn't have been in the newspaper this morning. She prayed Jimmy hadn't seen it.

There was a knock on the door; it was Detective Fletcher. Megan watched as he kissed Samantha hello. He was smiling at her as though he was happy to see her. Jimmy never showed he was happy to see Megan, and he never asked her how her day was the way Detective Fletcher asked Samantha.

"My day was terrific; I now have an assistant," Samantha said, walking toward Megan. "You remember Megan Fairbanks."

Fletch was glad Samantha's workload would be eased.

"Megan, it's nice to see you again under better circumstances."

"Hello, Detective Fletcher. I'm very happy to be here."

"Call me Fletch. I was planning to take your boss to dinner; would you like to join us to celebrate your new job?"

"Oh, that would be very nice, but I have to get home." She turned to Samantha. "I'll be here at nine o'clock sharp unless you want me earlier."

"Nine o'clock will be perfect. I'll see you in the morning and thank you for all your help today."

*****

The door closed behind Megan.

"Do you think I made a mistake in hiring her?"

"No, she seems like a nice girl. It was quick, though. Are you having second thoughts?"

"I am, but not because of Megan. It's her boyfriend I worry about. I don't like him and I don't trust him. If Megan is working for me, I'm bound to see him, and I certainly don't want him in my home. I realized after I'd offered her the job that I probably should have run a background check on her."

"You can still do that. I'd like to run one on Jimmy too. I'll order both tomorrow morning. In the meantime, you can tell me all you know about Mrs. Forrest Wakefield while I nibble on that pretty neck of yours."

"I don't want to talk about the dreary Margaret Wakefield while you nibble. Shall we talk about her later?"

CHAPTER 6

"Good evening, First Lady of Lancashire."

"Forrest, you're finally home. We have plans to make for your inauguration. Come into my study; I have a preliminary draft ready. I have a call into Antonia Sparazo's agent. I wish he'd call me back; I want her to sing the national anthem. I've begun a list of dignitaries we will invite."

"Margaret, dear, there won't be an inauguration— with or without a party. I've already been sworn in. I'm acting mayor, nothing more. Why would you contact a famous opera singer to perform the national anthem? The position is mayor of Lancashire, not President of the United States."

"What do you mean you've been sworn in? I wasn't even there. How dare they exclude the first lady of the city?"

"Margaret, it was simply a formality; you weren't excluded. We can hardly have a celebration so soon after Richard's assassination."

"He wasn't assassinated; he was murdered. I know Sophia arranged for her husband to be killed, and who can blame her? He humiliated the poor woman for years traipsing around with one trollop after another while she pretended to be an actress."

"I don't understand why you dislike her so, Margaret. The woman never did you any harm."

"Because, you old fool, I was the one who should have been the first lady. If you'd had an ounce of ambition, you would be in Richard's place now."

"You mean I would be dead?"

"No, you idiot; you'd be a real mayor, and I'd be the first lady. A role I was born for."

"I didn't think anyone was *born* to be the first lady of Lancashire, but whatever you say, dear."

"Don't think you've heard the end of this, Forrest Wakefield. Maybe I'll have to postpone my plans for an inauguration, but we can still have a celebration. I'll book the country club right away."

"Margaret, you won't do any such thing. A man is dead and this is not the time for a party."

She stomped out of the room and Forrest knew it meant he would be preparing his own dinner. He poured himself a drink and opened the refrigerator, hoping to find a couple of slices of cheese. After another bourbon, a grilled cheese sandwich would hit the spot.

*****

"Eloise, do you think I'm a suspect in Richard's murder? I was performing when he was shot, but those detectives might think I hired someone to kill Richard. Not that it wouldn't be justifiable homicide."

"You are *not* capable of murder—when you are yourself. Tell me, Sophia, when was the last time you had an episode?"

"I don't remember, but they're coming more often. Maybe I did hire someone to kill Richard. Oh, Eloise, how could I do such a thing?"

"I'm sure you didn't, my dear. You couldn't hurt a fly."

Other than her doctor, Eloise was the only person who was aware that Sophia was experiencing episodes of sleepwalking. Dr. Peters had run several tests and couldn't find any neurological reason for them. He encouraged Sophia to seek the help of a psychiatrist but she'd refused. She didn't know much about her family's history, but her mother had always said: 'Uncle Timothy is crazy as a loon.' He was a family joke but it was not funny to Sophia because she adored her uncle.

Sophia's episodes always happened in the evening. She would be sitting on the sofa, reading a script or a book and the next thing she knew, it was morning and she was climbing out of bed. It could be she had simply fallen asleep, but she remembered seeing a movie about someone with multiple personality disorder and was afraid that might be what was happening to her.

*****

The pasta was just about perfect for Fletch's taste. He liked it just slightly overcooked.

"Al dente is for the upper class," he would say. "I'm just a lowly cop who doesn't like my spaghetti crunchy."

Samantha's dad always liked it that way too and she was used to it.

"I hope you don't mind staying in tonight. I picked up some marina sauce at Benivitto's and I'm anxious to try it."

"It smells terrific and so do you."

"Don't start that again or we'll never eat."

Fletch poured the wine while Samantha took the piping hot garlic bread out of the oven.

"You were going to tell me what you know about Margaret Wakefield."

"Yes. I don't know her well, but my experiences with her have been far from pleasant. She's the leader of a woman's group at the Country Club. They meet once a month and usually have a speaker. It normally is someone who has knowledge of local history. I was invited because of my association with Professor Stonehill. Margaret Wakefield is the most condescending woman I've ever known. I think she resented that I'd only known the professor for a matter of months.

"I talked about my book and answered questions. Everyone in the room seemed interested in what I had to say, that is, except Margaret Wakefield. She interrupted me several times with her interpretation of the professor's words.

"Most of the women in the audience seemed reluctant to speak up, except Agatha Cromwell. Agatha finally looked at Margaret and said: 'Sit down and listen. You might learn something, Maggie.'

"Margaret never uttered a peep after that, she simply glared at me until the end of my presentation. It was very uncomfortable.

"Several of the women approached me later and apologized for Margaret's behavior. While I was gathering my materials, I noticed she was downright nasty to the people who were cleaning and straightening the room after everyone left. Maybe she was just having a bad day, but my instincts tell me she's always a bit difficult."

*****

Megan Fairbanks was keeping dinner warm in the oven while waiting for Jimmy to come home. She was nervous about what his reaction would be concerning the picture in *The Globe* that morning. Her only hope was that he hadn't seen it at the newsstand around the corner. She was tempted to call her mother, but Jimmy didn't like her talking to her family unless he was in the room.

She thought back to being in Samantha's apartment when Fletch came in. They looked at each other with such love in their eyes. Jimmy never looked at her in that way; he never seemed to look at her at all anymore. When she'd met him, it was love at first sight. He was exciting with an edge, unlike any boy she'd ever known. Her parents didn't approve of him, but that made him even more irresistible to her.

Her mother and father begged her to break it off with him.

"He's going to break your heart, Megan; we don't want you to be hurt."

After telling Jimmy what her parents had said, he informed her he was moving to Lancashire. "You can come with me or stay in this rinky dink town with mommy and daddy."

She packed a bag and left a note for her parents. She was afraid they'd talk her out of going with Jimmy if she faced them.

She hadn't seen her family in six months and missed them. Jimmy was out almost every night; she never knew where he was or who he was with.

*****

Jimmy was at his favorite watering hole that evening. He didn't drink often but he needed a couple of beers to take the edge off. His boss was coming down hard on him. It wasn't fair; he worked harder than the others but he wasn't getting the respect he deserved. What he did wasn't always legal, but Jimmy didn't care. If some dopey kid got hooked on drugs, what did he care? As long as there was money in selling them, his services would be needed. He pictured himself as the boss someday. That way he could sit back and rake it in. Maybe he'd even keep Megan with him; she was a good cook and he liked to eat.

He didn't like that she was with that guy who was killed the night before. He had to admit, he hadn't been listening closely when she'd told him about it. If he'd given any serious thought to Megan going out with some guy, he'd have put a stop to it.

His buddy, Butch Edgar, sat down beside him.

"Hey, Jimmy, that was a nice picture of your old lady in the paper. How come you let her go out with the mayor? I should say, the dead mayor."

"What are you talking about, Butch?"

"It's in *The Globe*—your woman as big as life with the mayor's hands all over her."

Jimmy threw some money on the bar and drank the rest of his beer in one swallow. He slammed the bottle down and stormed out the door. He stopped at the drugstore across the street. They still had a copy of *The Globe* in front of the counter. There was Megan, looking like a tramp. He grabbed the paper and walked out. The clerk didn't notice him until she saw his backside in the doorway. She let him leave; it was only a newspaper and he was too big to risk trying to stop him for a one dollar item.

Megan heard him open the door when he came in. She jumped up to greet him as he slammed the paper on the coffee table.

"What's this? I thought you said that jerk didn't try anything. You two look pretty cozy to me."

"I don't know how they got that picture, but it's not real. Haven't you ever heard of Photoshop, Jimmy?"

"It looks real to me. When were you going to tell me your picture is all over the front page? You humiliated me, Megan."

He made a fist and she backed up, falling, and hitting her side on the edge of the coffee table. She cried out in pain but he ignored her.

CHAPTER 7

The next morning, Megan arrived at Samantha's apartment promptly at nine o'clock.

"Are you feeling all right, Megan? You look tired this morning."

"I'm fine, but I didn't sleep well last night." She winced taking off her sweater.

"I'd say it was more than lack of sleep; are you hurt?"

"I fell last night and hit my side on the coffee table; it doesn't hurt that much."

"Did you fall or were you pushed?" Samantha asked.

"I fell," she said emphatically. "I'd better get to work and finish what I started yesterday."

Samantha wanted to pursue the matter further, but sensed that Megan had nothing more she wanted to say. She was certain Jimmy had something to do with her fall.

There was a knock on the door. "Samantha, it's Mike."

"Mike, welcome home. I didn't expect to see you until next week."

"I got in late last night. It was a successful trip; the company liked my ideas and I'll be doing the job for them. I wanted to thank Fletch for the heads up. His friend, Arnie, was most helpful."

"I'm happy it worked out for you. Come in and meet my new assistant, Megan Fairbanks. Megan, this is my neighbor and good friend, Mike Thompson; he just got back from Chicago."

"Hello, Megan. I'm happy to meet you. Samantha has needed an assistant for months now. I'm glad she has someone to help her out."

"It's nice to meet you too, Mike. Did you say you'll be working in Chicago?"

"No, I'm an architect and designed a building for a friend Fletch put me in contact with. I'll be going back and forth, but I'm a lifelong resident of Lancashire and don't plan to move away any time soon."

"I don't blame you; it's a beautiful city. My boyfriend and I have only been here a few months but I feel at home here."

Samantha could see the disappointment in Mike's eyes when he heard the word *boyfriend*. Her cupid instincts kicked in and she couldn't help but think what a cute couple these two would make.

Samantha walked Mike out into the hallway.

"Now I have two beautiful women as neighbors. If they weren't both taken, I'd be a lucky guy."

"Megan is very sweet. I'm not sure about that boyfriend of hers; he's a bully and I don't trust him."

"You seem to have good instincts about people. Remember, if you ever need any help, I'm just across the hall."

"Thanks, Mike; would you like to come back for lunch? Fletch bought enough cheese and ham from the deli yesterday to feed an army."

"I'll take you up on it. Will Fletch be here? I'd like to thank him personally for the referral."

"He'll be here at noon unless something breaks in the Delaney murder. If that happens, I won't see him for hours or days."

Samantha watched as Megan worked diligently. She was a good worker and a nice young woman. She and Mike would be good together. *Mind your own business, Samantha.*

Her phone rang and it was Fletch.

"Hello, beautiful, are you alone?"

"I can be," she said, walking into the bedroom. "What's up?"

"I ran those background checks. Megan is as clean as a whistle. Jimmy Lee Butler, however, has an extensive record. Mostly petty stuff, but he was arrested for an alleged beating of a woman. The victim refused to testify and the case was dismissed. He's been involved in the alleged selling of drugs but never convicted. If the guy has ever held down a job, there's no record of it. He's a loser, Samantha. I don't feel comfortable with him having access to you through Megan."

"It's worse than I thought. I'll talk to Megan and probably let her go. I don't want to lose her, but I will not allow Jimmy in this apartment and she will undoubtedly choose him over her job."

"Good luck and I'll see you at lunch."

Samantha dreaded talking to Megan. She suspected she was a victim of verbal abuse, and now with the knowledge that Jimmy had presumably beaten a woman and the fact that Megan had obviously been injured last night, she was convinced her suspicions were correct.

"Megan, why don't you take a break and come sit with me for a minute?"

"Is there something wrong, Samantha? Have I made a mistake?"

"No, it's nothing about your work. This is not easy for me to say, but I don't feel comfortable having Jimmy in my apartment. Fletch ran a background check on him and it turns out he has a record of criminal activity."

"Oh, but that was a long time ago when he was just a kid. He's told me all about the mischief he and his friends got into when they were teenagers."

"It's more than high school pranks, Megan. Did you know he was arrested for beating a woman? The charges were later dropped. Did he ever hurt you physically?"

"No."

"Did he ever push you or raise his fist to you?"

"He never pushed me. I swear, Samantha."

Megan began to cry.

"Tell me why your side is hurting. Have you been injured?"

Megan lifted her shirt to expose a swollen and deeply bruised area around her ribs.

"It was my fault; I fell on the coffee table. Jimmy didn't touch me."

"Megan, you might not like what I'm going to say, but I took a class in school about those who abuse women and children. I learned of the progression of abuse. It starts when the abuser begins to alienate the victim from her family and friends. He will belittle the person he professes to love until she no longer feels she has any worth. Eventually, he begins to become physically abusive. It might start as a little push or shove. He might even simply raise his fist to show he's boss. After a while, those little shoves become bigger shoves and the clenched fist finally hits its target. The abuser is usually apologetic after the fact, but blames his victim for provoking him. Does this sound like your relationship with Jimmy?"

Megan looked at Samantha with tears streaming down her face.

"All those things you said are true. Jimmy won't let me call any of my old friends. He allows only a five-minute call once a week to my parents and he insists on being in the room when I talk to them. I feel so alone; I have no one to talk to. I thought I loved him but now

I'm simply afraid of him. Oh, Samantha, I've ruined my life."

"You might have made some poor choices, Megan, but you haven't ruined your life. The first step is to move out of the apartment you share with Jimmy. Are you willing to do that?"

"I don't think he'll let me and I don't know where I'd go. I can't afford to live on my own."

"Do you think your parents would be willing to have you move back home with them?"

"I don't know; they were awfully mad at me when I ran away with Jimmy."

"You could stay here for a while until you decide where you want to go. There isn't much room in the office, but I'm sure we could find some space for a bed for you."

"I couldn't impose on you like that."

"Nothing has to be decided now. Why don't we both get back to work? Fletch and Mike will be here for lunch; we can discuss this again after they leave."

"Thank you, Samantha. I feel like you're my only friend."

They both got back to work. Samantha had a difficult time concentrating. She was worried about Megan and her fear of Jimmy was growing as she wondered what he would do if Megan left him.

CHAPTER 8

Shortly before noon, Samantha set the table for lunch. She and Megan prepared a big plate of sandwiches. Fletch and Mike arrived at the same time.

"Where's Robin? I thought you were going to bring her along," said Samantha.

"She had a thing at school for one of the kids and asked for a rain check," said Fletch.

The four of them talked and laughed until every sandwich had disappeared. Megan hadn't felt this relaxed in a very long time.

Suddenly, they heard a banging on the door. Megan's heart skipped a beat and the color drained from her face. She heard a familiar voice shouting from the hallway.

"Let me in or I'll break the door down."

Fletch stood up and slowly walked to the door, opening it up to reveal an outraged Jimmy.

"So, this is your new job? It doesn't look like work to me. Who's this bozo?" he said, glaring at Mike.

Mike was not perturbed by the comment and held out his hand.

"I'm Mike Thompson. I live across the hall. Samantha was kind enough to invite me to lunch."

"Yeah, Samantha is really good at stickin' her nose where it doesn't belong. Why'd you give this job to a dummy like Megan? Are you trying to cause trouble?"

"That's enough, Jimmy," said Fletch. "Calm down and let's take a walk outside."

"I'm not leaving here without Megan."

"I'm not going with you, Jimmy. I have more work to do. Please leave and we'll talk later this evening, that is, if you choose to come home before midnight."

Mike thanked Samantha for lunch and walked across the hall to his apartment. He thought it best to leave because his presence might be interpreted the wrong way by Megan's boyfriend. He was sorry the lunch had been interrupted as he was enjoying himself. Megan was a nice girl, too nice for a jerk like Jimmy.

Fletch managed to calm Jimmy down. He walked him to the front door of the building and warned him not to make trouble for Megan and Samantha. He then went back to the apartment.

"Megan, do you want me to stay for a while to make sure he doesn't come back?"

"No, Fletch, I don't think he will. He gets mad but cools off quickly."

He gave her his card. "Call me anytime; I'll be here or at your apartment in a matter of minutes."

Fletch left the women alone to finish their workday. He didn't feel comfortable with Jimmy being free to roam the streets of Lancashire. He didn't have a choice. The guy was obnoxious, but hadn't done anything illegal—so far.

*****

"When is that woman going to schedule her husband's funeral?" Margaret Wakefield fumed at Forrest. "I can't live in limbo forever."

"No one is asking you to live in limbo, Margaret. Our lives won't be much different from what they've been all along."

"Forrest, I am First Lady of Lancashire. There is a vast difference between me and the former first lady. That woman never did deserve the title."

"I have never been able to understand your dislike of Sophia Delaney. When has the woman ever been anything but gracious to you?"

"Forrest, you are a typical man. You can't look beyond a pretty face and an enlarged bust line. You don't think those things are real, do you?"

"I don't know, nor do I care. There must be more to your negative feelings than her looks. You can be a harsh woman, Margaret."

"You would never understand, Forrest. It doesn't matter because she and that sex maniac husband of hers will be gone from our lives the day he's buried in Lakeside Cemetery."

Forrest cringed at his wife's coldness. It was true, he'd never be in the place he was in today if it hadn't been for Margaret. She wasn't satisfied that her husband was the head of a prestigious accounting firm. She'd pushed him into accepting the position of deputy mayor. He had to admit, it had worked out well for him. Now that Richard was no longer in the picture, there was no telling where Forrest's destination would be. He'd been humming the tune of *Hail to the Chief* since the day he'd been informed of Mayor Delaney's demise.

*****

"Sophia, arrangements are finalized. Richard's funeral will be tomorrow morning at Saint Augustine's Church. It's time to say goodbye, dear."

"Thank you, Eloise. I could never have done this on my own. Don't you think Saint Augustine's might be bit hypocritical? It's the largest and most esteemed house of worship in Lancashire. You and I both know Richard hadn't stepped inside a church in his entire adult life."

"Hypocrisy and politics go hand in hand, my dear. Now, it's time to try on the dresses Winslow's

Department Store sent over for your approval. You want to look your best and make Richard proud."

"Richard was never proud of me when he was alive; why would he start now?"

*****

"Hello, Samantha, is it quiet over there? You haven't heard from Jimmy Lee again, have you?"

"No, Fletch. Megan says he's probably off sulking somewhere. I hope she gets out of that relationship soon. I worry about her. By the way, she and Mike seemed to hit it off, don't you think?"

"It looked that way to me, and, unfortunately, to Jimmy too, I'm afraid. I'm not condoning his reaction but I do understand it."

"He's the type of jerk who doesn't want the girl unless someone else does. I worry that he'll come back again. I don't want him hanging around my apartment."

"Maybe I should plan to move in for a while. I can be your personal rent-a-cop. No charge, of course."

"I've already told Megan she can bunk here. It would be a tight squeeze for the three of us."

"I don't mind tight squeezes, especially when you're involved. The other reason I called is to let you know Mayor Delaney's funeral is tomorrow morning. I thought we could go together, that is, if you'd like to go at all."

"I think I should go. I'll tell Megan to come in after one o'clock tomorrow. That should give us plenty of time for the funeral and reception. Will I see you later?"

"I'm here until about eight. Do you mind if I check in with you on the way to my lonely apartment?"

"I don't mind at all."

After Samantha's call ended, she talked to Megan about the funeral and coming in later in the day.

"Do you think I should go to the funeral?"

"Only if you want to, Megan. I'm sure there will be reporters there and I know you don't want to have any encounters with them."

"I'd rather not face reporters. I'll take some time in the morning to pack up my things. While you were on the phone, I called my mother. She and Daddy are wiring me money to put down on an apartment of my own. Mom cried when I told her I was planning to leave Jimmy. I feel guilty because I made them worry about me."

"Do you know where you will live?"

"No, I was hoping there was a studio apartment available in this building. I don't need much room."

"Let's talk to the superintendent—that is, if you're sure. I don't want to rush your decision."

"You aren't rushing me at all. I think I made up my mind to do this weeks ago. I just didn't have the courage to tell my parents I'd made a mistake."

*****

"Good news, Margaret, Richard's funeral will be tomorrow morning."

"Tomorrow? I can't possibly be ready by tomorrow. I must get my hair done and find a suitable outfit to wear, and just look at my nails—they're a mess! Oh, Forrest, that woman is the bane of my existence."

Forrest shook his head and walked away. There was no pleasing that woman. He wondered why he put up with her nonsense, but he knew, in spite of everything, he loved her. He loved her so much he would gladly do almost anything to make her happy.

*****

Samantha and Megan visited the rental office of the apartment building. A furnished studio apartment was available on the first floor. Unfortunately, they wouldn't be able to rent it to Megan without a background check that would take a minimum of a week. The super had a slight crush on Samantha and when she offered to vouch for Megan, he waived the waiting period. Megan could move in any time.

Samantha wrote a check for the deposit and first month's rent. Megan would be able to pay her back when her parent's money arrived.

Megan was nervous driving to the apartment she shared with Jimmy and relieved that he wasn't home.

After she collected her things and locked them in the trunk of her car, she decided to have one more look through the apartment. She didn't want to forget anything because it would be awkward to return. The note she'd left on the kitchen counter was waiting for Jimmy's return.

Jimmy,
It isn't working for us and I'm leaving.
I hope you will find someone who makes
you happy. It's obvious I don't.
Megan

It wasn't much of an explanation, but Megan knew Jimmy wouldn't care why she was leaving. He would be mad but he'd get over it. She didn't want to tell him that he'd embarrassed her this afternoon with his behavior. She was having the best time she'd had in months until he barged in and ruined everything.

What a fool she'd been when she let him talk her into leaving her home and her family. He'd said they would be going to California. That was months ago, and he hadn't mentioned it again. She was happy they ended up in Lancashire and she didn't want to leave. Jimmy could go off to California if he wanted, but she would stay right here.

The door opened and he surprised her.

"If it isn't the town tramp," he bellowed. "It didn't take you long to get over your boyfriend—the dead mayor—and now you've latched onto someone else."

He raised his fist and swung it at her. Megan ducked and he hit his hand on the doorway.

That made him madder than he already was. He swung and missed again.

"Jimmy, you're drunk. When you sober up, you can read my note. In the meantime, I'm leaving and you can't stop me."

"You aren't going anywhere; no one leaves Jimmy Lee Butler."

He grabbed her arm and threw her down on the floor. Megan was stunned; she tried to get up but he held her down with his foot on her chest. At that moment, she knew what real fear was. His eyes were filled with hate.

"Jimmy, please don't hurt me."

"I should kill you and then you'll be with your boyfriend, rotting in Hell."

"Jimmy, you have to believe me, I don't have a boyfriend; you're the only one, I promise."

Megan was shocked when Jimmy began to sob. She had never seen him like this before.

"Oh, baby. I don't want you to leave. I can't live without you. Please give me another chance. I'll be good, I promise. I'll never hit you again."

Although her arm was throbbing, she held Jimmy while he continued to cry like a baby. She reluctantly told him she'd stay with him that night. He finally passed out.

She reached into his pocket and found several pills. She wondered what he'd taken and whether they, mixed with alcohol, were the reason he was acting like a crazy person.

Megan left Jimmy sleeping on the floor. She brought his pillow from the bed and a blanket. She wouldn't be able to move him to the bed if she tried.

I'll sleep on the couch tonight. There's no way I'll get into our bed with or without him. I'll just make sure he's all right until morning and then I'll leave.

Megan slept fitfully through the night, her arm was painful and bruised, but it wasn't broken.

CHAPTER 9

Cindy Matthews applied a third coat of foundation below her eyes in an attempt to hide the puffiness. She had cried her heart out since that horrible day when Richard had said her services were no longer needed.

Cindy began working for the newly-elected mayor the day he took office. She'd been executive assistant to the university president when Richard Delaney gave a speech in the auditorium. Cindy thought he was the most beautiful man she'd ever seen. She began working tirelessly on his campaign while never shirking her responsibilities at the university. By the time she discovered Richard had a wife, it was too late; she had fallen in love.

At first, Richard treated her as he did every pretty girl, with just a hint of flirtation. However, as the campaign wore on and she made herself available, he began to take notice.

The people of Lancashire took the office of mayor seriously and Richard obliged. After a Saturday filled with speeches and town hall meetings, he asked Cindy to join him for a late supper at an inn outside of town. There, e asked her to head up his staff and she quickly accepted his offer.

For the first several months after Richard's election, Cindy accompanied him to the many social affairs the mayor attended. Quite often, Cindy was mistaken for the first lady. After a while, she stopped correcting the mistake. She enjoyed being thought of as Mayor

Delaney's wife and began thinking of herself as his wife too.

*****

Her bubble burst the day Eloise Kittredge paid her a visit.

"Cindy, my dear," Eloise said condescendingly. "It is becoming obvious that you have fallen for the charms of the mayor, and that will never do. He will be attending an informal gathering of supporters this evening. You will make an excuse why you won't be there."

"But, Eloise, I promised Richard I would be with him."

"You can find another young woman for him to escort; he prefers blondes. I suggest you find one and make it snappy."

And so, it began—the long progression of pretty young women on Richard's arm. Cindy wondered what his wife thought about her husband always being seen with another female, but she tried not to think about his wife. She had met Sophia a few times and had liked her but she still hoped to take her place someday.

Cindy was content to wait for her someday with Richard and was shocked when he called her into his office just a week ago.

"Cindy, I will be announcing my intention to run for governor of our state in a few short weeks. I will be needing an executive assistant."

"Sir, I will be happy to follow you to the capitol."

"I appreciate that, but I will need someone more suited to the prestigious position of executive assistant to the governor. I'm sure you understand."

It took every bit of self control that Cindy could muster to smile and walk away. She was heartbroken. The man she loved with all her heart was tossing her aside because she wasn't suitable enough for the office of the governor.

I could kill him, she thought to herself. *If I had a knife, I'd go in there and plunge it firmly into his unfeeling heart. Maybe I'll poison his coffee with arsenic. That's how they do it in old movies. I hear it's a painful way to die. Oh, Richard, how could you do this to me?*

Somehow, she made it through the day, and the days that followed. All the while, she was plotting a way to make Richard Delaney suffer just as she was suffering.

*****

"Eloise, what do you think of this dress? Too much décolletage for a funeral?" laughed Sophia.

"Not too much, dear. I do believe Richard would approve. My, but you're in a good mood this morning."

"You know how I love dressing for a performance. I can hardly wait to be on stage."

"Sophia, you realize you're going to Richard's funeral and not a presentation of *The Music Man*."

"Of course, I know that. I'm telling myself it's only a performance; it can't be real because that would mean Richard is dead and I don't want to believe he's gone."

"Did you have a sleepwalking incident last night?"

"You know I can't remember them. For all I know, I'm asleep now."

Sophia couldn't bear the look of pity in Eloise's eyes. She wondered if Eloise was suspicious of her. Sophia had known some shady characters in her day. She could think of several who might kill if the monetary reward was worth the risk.

It wasn't long ago that she'd had a dream that she was watching from the sidelines when a bullet pierced into Richard's head. Was it a dream or reality? She had a hard time lately distinguishing between the two. She knew exactly where Richard would be sitting the night he was shot. She'd reserved the seat herself.

*****

Jimmy woke up and realized he'd slept all night on the floor. He had a pillow under his head and a blanket covering his upper body. He remembered throwing back a few beers and a couple of shots. He reached into his pocket and pulled out several pills. His head was throbbing and it was all that uptight bitch's fault. *Ever since Megan met Samantha Degan, she's been a real pain. First, she's all over the mayor and yesterday she was cozy with that guy at Degan's apartment.*

He forced himself to stand up and walked to the bathroom for something to stop the throbbing in his head. He didn't often have more than a couple of beers because too much booze made him crave speed. Last night they didn't give him the euphoria he usually experienced, and today he was sick as a dog. The more he thought of Samantha Degan, the madder he got. He threw himself on the bed and passed out thinking of ways he could make her pay for ruining his happy life.

*****

Samantha looked through her closet for something subdued to wear to the funeral. Since she'd met Fletch her choice of outfits had reflected her joyful mood. She did have one dress she hadn't worn since her interview with Professor Stonehill. Her life had changed dramatically since that day. She was now a published author with a calendar filled with speaking engagements. Of course, her celebrity had more to do with the subject of her book than her writing skill, but she was beginning to feel more comfortable being the center of attention. She was madly in love with the detective who'd arrested her for Professor Stonehill's murder, and he loved her. The only thing that cast a shadow over her, otherwise, total happiness was the death of the mayor. Fletch was frustrated that there were no significant leads in the case. She wished she could help him solve the murder. Maybe she'd have a chance to talk with some of the people who knew the victim. Someone might unknowingly have information that would be beneficial in solving the crime.

*****

Megan Fairbanks let herself into her new studio apartment. She couldn't believe the turn her life had taken in just a few days. She felt a strong sense of relief to know she was free of Jimmy Lee Butler for the last time. She'd been a fool to put up with him for as long as she had. Thanks to Samantha, she'd finally found the courage to leave him and his control.

It took two trips back and forth to her car, but she was finally unpacked. Her clothes were hung neatly in the closet and the dresser drawers next to the bed were filled. There was a small kitchenette with empty cupboards. She hadn't eaten anything yet today. She'd left the apartment before Jimmy woke up. Megan wondered if he was still sleeping on the floor, but knew he wasn't any longer her concern.

There was a knock on the door. Her heart skipped a beat. Could Jimmy have found her already?

"Megan, it's Mike Thompson. We met yesterday at Samantha Degan's place."

Megan quickly opened the door. Mike was standing there with a tray of coffee and piping hot breakfast sandwiches.

"I thought you might be ready for a break."

"Mike, you are heaven-sent. I haven't had my morning coffee yet. Please come in and sit down."

Megan took a sip of the warm drink and bit into the sandwich.

"How did you know I was here?"

"I saw the super on the elevator. That guy knows everything that goes on here, and he likes to share his knowledge with anyone and everyone."

"Maybe I'd better ask him not to share too much with Jimmy Butler."

"Doesn't he know you're here?"

"No, I left him a note but he was so drunk and out of it last night, he's probably still sleeping it off."

"I'm sorry you have to go through that, Megan."

"Thanks, Mike. I'm fine now. I was a fool to ever fall for his line in the first place. It's over now, and I don't regret leaving. Tell me about yourself, Mike. A good-looking guy like you must have all the female companionship you can handle."

"There are so many I have to beat them off with a stick," he laughed. "Actually, I recently went through a breakup up myself."

"I'm sorry to hear that."

"It's not so bad. We had drifted apart for several months before the breakup. There was a time when we talked of marriage. It's a good thing we discovered we weren't right for each other before we tied the knot. I have no regrets. I shouldn't keep you any longer; I have work to do. I just wanted to welcome you to the building, neighbor."

"Thanks, Mike, and thanks for breakfast. Once I get to the supermarket, I'll invite you for dinner to reciprocate."

"That's not necessary, but I would like that. By the way, would you consider working for me one day a week? I don't have too much clerical work, but it would help me out if you have the time."

"That would be great. I can sure use the money. I borrowed from my parents to move into this place and I'd like to pay them back as quickly as possible."

"Good, we'll work your hours around Samantha's schedule."

Megan closed the door after he left. *What a great guy! I wish I'd met someone like him instead of Jimmy. I'm being ridiculous; he's just looking for friendship and I'm in no shape to start another relationship. I'll be happy to have him as a friend and a boss.*

CHAPTER 10

The church was filled with mourners and those who were there to see and be seen. Sophia looked around and saw many of her friends from the theater. She wasn't particularly close to any of her co-stars but she liked them and they liked her. She had taken great pains to portray herself as the grieving widow and it was well worth the trouble. She said and did all the right things; she happily posed for photos before and after the ceremony.

Eloise planned a reception in the church community room, knowing Sophia would not want a large formal gathering. Her nerves would begin to crumble after a few hours and the poor thing would never be able to stay in control.

Sophia was shocked when Margaret Wakefield approached her and said she had arranged for a reception at the country club.

"A church basement is no place to honor the mayor of Lancashire. I have Richard's staff spreading the word. We will expect you after the burial Sophia; you will be seated at the head table, of course."

Sophia wasn't sure how long she would be able to keep up the performance of her life.

*****

Samantha glanced across the aisle of the church and noticed a young woman crying from the moment she sat down.

Turning to Robin, she asked, "Do you know who that woman is?"

"Cindy Matthews," Robin replied, "Mayor Delaney's executive assistant. I have the feeling she was half in love with him, but a lot of women felt the same way."

"He was a pretty smooth character," said Samantha.

"More like a slick character, I'd say. A little too slick for my taste. I like an unpretentious guy like Fletch and my Frank," said Robin.

"Mrs. Delaney looks like a movie star. If she's grieving her husband, she's hiding it well," said Samantha.

"She *is* a beautiful woman," noted Robin. "I've only seen pictures of her in the newspaper. I was on duty when the mayor was inaugurated."

"You were lucky," whispered Fletch. "It was required that most of the force be there; it was a cold and windy day in January. I didn't think his speech would ever end. Sofia looked like a Russian princess."

"I remember pictures of her outfit," added Robin. "Samantha, she wore a snow-white coat with a white fur collar, a matching fur hat, and carried a fur muff. Who carries a muff in this century? Fletch is right; she did look like a Russian princess. Do they have princesses in Russia anymore? I wonder who that lady is with her?"

"That's Eloise Kittredge," responded Samantha. "I think someone said she was Richard's campaign manager. She's very close to Sophia; I wonder what the story is there." Samantha's writer's curiosity was getting the best of her. "I see the Acting First Lady is taking over the show. Margaret Wakefield has finally found her calling in life."

"That's Forrest Wakefield's wife?" Robin asked. "I expected a mousy little gray-haired woman. Poor Forrest. I don't think he's much of a match for her; she looks like the bossy type."

"Believe me, she is," Samantha concurred.

"Are you two having fun?" laughed Frank. "Maybe we should separate them, Fletch, before they get us thrown out of here for gossiping in a church."

"We aren't gossiping, Frank; we're simply exchanging information. Samantha's a mystery writer collecting ideas for her new book."

The sounds of *Ave Maria* sung by the University of Lancashire's A Capella Choir signaled the beginning of the funeral service.

After eulogies were given, music played and prayers said, acting Mayor Wakefield held Sophia's arm as he guided her out of the church. Frank was a few eye blinks away from dozing off when he felt Robin's hand on his arm indicating the service had ended and his torture was over.

The foursome walked slowly up the aisle, waiting their turn to offer condolences to Mayor Delaney's widow. When they finally reached the steps of the church, Samantha realized she'd left her sweater behind in the pew.

"I'll be back in a minute," she said as she walked back into the sanctuary.

After she retrieved her sweater, she saw a woman's head bowed and could hear muffled sobs. Samantha knew it was none of her business, but felt compelled to offer comfort.

Cindy Matthews looked up, sensing someone was standing by her.

"Is there anything I can do to help?" asked Samantha.

"No, I wanted to be alone with Richard one last time. I know I'm making a terrible fool of myself," Cindy said between sobs.

"You aren't a fool at all. I'm sure you were very close to your boss; it's natural that you're mourning his sudden death."

"You're Samantha Degan, aren't you? After reading your book about Professor Stonehill, I feel as though I knew him personally. You knew how to capture the essence of the man."

"Thank you; that's a lovely compliment. Would you like me to leave you alone or would you like to talk about your feelings?"

"I'll be all right. I need to get to the reception before Mrs. Wakefield notices I'm not where I should be. She gave me strict instructions to sit at a designated table with the rest of the worker bees, as she so disdainfully put it."

"Mrs. Wakefield is a bit of a challenge, isn't she?"

"You're being too kind; she's a royal pain in the neck. I feel sorry for the others who must put up with her. I'm glad I won't be a part of it."

"Won't you stay on as the mayor's assistant?"

"No, Wanda Anderson has that job now, she'd never step aside. I haven't told anyone this, but Richard gave me my walking papers before he died. He had plans to run for governor and felt he needed someone more suitable as his executive assistant."

The tears started again and Samantha put her arm around Cindy until she calmed down. They walked out of the church together. Cindy was glad to have someone to talk to. Dare she tell her new friend how much she wanted Richard Delaney to pay for breaking her heart?

*****

The reception at the country club was underway. Margaret Wakefield had outdone herself. *If only I'd had more time to plan,* she thought. *Just look at the grieving widow; I knew that marriage was doomed. After today, neither the City of Lancashire nor I will have to look at that insipid face again.*

Sophia looked around the room at the waiters passing out glasses of champagne and fancy appetizers. *Richard would have loved this, it's too bad he didn't marry someone like Margaret Wakefield. She does know how to throw a party, although the funeral of my husband is hardly a time for celebration. I despise this kind of thing, with all these people. I'll just go on pretending this is a play and I'm performing my part.*

*****

"This is quite the affair; wouldn't you say, Samantha?" asked Robin. "I've heard the new First Lady is good at throwing a party, but this bash exceeds my expectations."

"The new First Lady also knows how to make people feel uncomfortable," Samantha replied. "I was watching Mrs. Delaney; it looks like her smile is painted on her face. I get the idea she's miserable being here. The former mayor's staff has been relegated to a table by the kitchen. Forrest just sits there with his chest puffed out; I think he's enjoying his new status."

"He's also enjoying his third scotch," said Fletch.

"I've noticed that too," replied Frank. "Why don't we pass on the champagne and head to the bar? It looks like they're open for business."

"Good idea; would you girls like something?"

"No thanks, Fletch. I'm enjoying the bubbly." Samantha winked at him.

"Nothing for me. Do you remember my condition?" said Robin, pointing to her swollen belly.

As the men walked to the bar, Margaret Wakefield glared at them and at the others who followed their lead. *I wish there was some way I could have avoided having all these ruffians here today,* she thought, unaware that her husband was being served another scotch.

Wanda Anderson was watching her boss; she knew he often swallowed a shot or two of whiskey before a meeting. It was simply to fortify him and give him the courage he needed to carry out his duties. Today she was worried. She counted the times he'd been served drinks and could see patches of red on his cheeks. She wanted to go to him and reassure him that everything would be all right, but with Mrs. Wakefield in the room, she knew that would not be a good idea. That woman didn't understand the pressure she put on Forrest to be something he wasn't. The man hated the spotlight. When he got a little tipsy in the office one time, he confided in Wanda that he preferred the old days when he was simply an accountant and had to deal with numbers instead of people.

*****

Eloise Kittredge found her way to Samantha's table.

"Ms. Degan, I don't know if you remember me; I'm a friend of Sophia Delaney."

"Yes, Eloise, of course, I remember you; please call me Samantha."

"Thank you, Samantha. I wonder if I could impose on you to check on Sophia. She went to the ladies' room a good ten minutes ago and hasn't returned to her seat. If I walk too far away from my table, I'm afraid Mrs. Wakefield will catch me and assign a task to me."

Samantha didn't understand the hold Margaret Wakefield seemed to have over everyone, but said she would be happy to check on Mrs. Delaney.

Inside the ladies' room, Sophia was sitting on a sofa at the rear of the lounge area. She stared into space and Samantha was wary approaching her.

"Mrs. Delaney, are you all right?"

Sophia looked into Samantha's eyes and said: "Did he love you too?"

"I beg your pardon?"

Sophia shook her head and blinked her eyes. "Hello, Samantha, did you say something to me?"

Samantha looked at her questioningly. "I asked if you were all right?"

"Yes, I'm afraid I dozed off for a few minutes. I'm sorry, I know I should have stayed in my seat but I couldn't bear watching Margaret Wakefield flaunting herself and her new role all over the room. Richard isn't even buried yet and that woman has taken over. Don't get me wrong, I never wanted to be the first lady of Lancashire, but Richard would be upset if he could see how she's acting."

"You make a lovely first lady. Don't let Margaret Wakefield get under your skin."

"You mean I'm playing my part well. I don't want to be here; I'd rather be home all by myself. I often wonder why Richard married me. I must have played a part back then because we never did have anything in common. I know he was a scoundrel, but I did love him."

"I'm sure he loved you in his way," said Samantha, although she wasn't sure of that at all. "You're a beautiful and warm woman, Sophia. Mayor Delaney was a lucky man to have you by his side."

"I like you, Samantha. You don't judge people, do you? I'd like to tell you something..."

The door flew open. "What are you doing in here, Sophia? There are people waiting to offer condolences and you are hiding in the women's lounge."

"Samantha and I were having a conversation, Margaret. I already accepted condolences at the church. I see no reason to stand there and listen to people gush over Richard again."

"Once again, you are proving to be the worst first lady Lancashire has ever known."

"I'm sure you will be the best, Margaret. It's a job you have wanted for years and now it's all yours. Wasn't it convenient of Richard to die so you could anoint yourself queen of Lancashire?"

Margaret looked in disgust at Sophia and glared at the two women. Samantha noticed a slight twitch in Margaret's eye. It was true that Richard's death was very convenient for an ambitious woman and her husband. The possible suspects in his murder were piling up in Samantha's mind.

"I'm sorry that witch disturbed us, Samantha. I'd like to continue our conversation sometime soon. Would you like to stop by the house in the next couple of days?"

"I'd like that, Sophia; let me know a good time and I'll be there."

Samantha wanted to hear what Sophia was about to tell her before Margaret Wakefield had burst into the room. She liked Sophia and suspected something was troubling her. She hoped she would feel comfortable confiding in her.

*****

"What was that all about?" asked Fletch.

"Eloise thought Sophia needed a friend. She's right; something's troubling her, and I'd like to find out what it is."

"Do you think she had something to do with Richard Delaney's death?"

Samantha didn't try to hide her concern. "I hope not," she whispered.

CHAPTER 11

It was shortly after one o'clock when Samantha returned to her apartment. Megan was already at work and on the telephone jotting down the details of a request for a speaking engagement.

"Your reputation is growing, Samantha. They want you as the keynote speaker for a hospital foundation luncheon in Middleton."

"Middleton? That's a three-hour drive from here. My grandparents had a cabin on the lake near there. Mom and Dad still go to Middleton a few times a year but it's vacant most of the time. I could spend a few days there and get some writing done without any distractions."

"Speaking of distractions, how was the funeral?"

"The funeral was lengthy. I thought we were going to lose Fletch and Frank halfway through. The reception at the country club was very interesting. Margaret Wakefield is trying to establish herself as the social leader of Lancashire and this was a very good start. Sophia Delaney was there only as window dressing."

"I think Sophia Delaney is a wonderful actress. Before the horrible shooting, I was having the time of my life watching her performance."

"She was performing today too. Tell me, how did it go last night? Did you tell Jimmy you were moving out?"

"Jimmy was in bad shape last night. He was drunk and acting weird. I almost felt sorry for him, but then I found some pills in his pocket. I don't know much about drugs, but I know I want nothing to do with anyone who does them. After he passed out, I was afraid to leave him alone. I fell asleep on the sofa and left first thing this morning."

Megan told Samantha about Mike bringing her breakfast and about her new part-time job with him.

"It's only one day a week and I'll make sure it doesn't interfere with my time with you."

"That's terrific. Mike is a great guy; I'm glad you two are friends."

"Yes, I am too. It's nice to have friends again, I haven't had any, except Jimmy, since we moved here. I know you're my boss, but I consider you my friend too."

"I'm glad you feel that way because I feel the same way too. I'm surprised Jimmy hasn't tried to contact you."

"Maybe that's a good sign; it could mean he's glad I'm gone." Megan held her crossed fingers in the air.

If she and Samantha looked out the window, they'd have seen Jimmy watching the apartment from across the street. *Nobody walks out on Jimmy Lee Butler.*

*****

Samantha answered her cell phone less than an hour after she returned home.

"Samantha, this is Sophia Delaney. I'm sure you're busy, but I was wondering if you'd be willing to meet with me this afternoon."

"Sophia, is everything all right? You don't sound like yourself."

"I'm sorry. I'm keeping my voice low because I don't want Eloise to know I'm asking to meet you. She'll want to join us and I'd rather she didn't."

"I understand," she said, although she didn't. "Where would you like to meet?"

"There's a coffee shop near the campus theater. It should be quiet this time of day. I can be there in twenty minutes. Eloise is napping; I'll be out of here before she wakes up."

Samantha knew the coffee shop well. One of her many part-time jobs while attending the university had been working there. She'd never been much of a coffee drinker but couldn't resist some of the chocolate-flavored, cream-filled options she'd made every day. By the end of the semester that year, she'd gained five pounds.

Samantha arrived at the coffee shop a few minutes early. For old-time sake, she ordered a mocha latté with extra cream. It was as good as she remembered.

Sophia came bustling through the door. She wore a tattered pair of jeans with an oversized shirt. Her hair was in a ponytail and she had only a touch of blush on her cheeks. She looked nothing like the glamorous actress who'd buried her husband just hours before.

"Thank you for meeting me, Samantha. I have the feeling you are someone I can talk to. I know you're friends with Detective Fletcher and I hope I'm not putting you in an uncomfortable position."

"Sophia, I'm happy to hear what you have to say, but if this has something to do with a police investigation, I must report our conversation."

"I understand; the thing is, I don't know if it has anything to do with Richard's murder. Eloise has told me not to mention my suspicions to anyone, but I can't keep quiet any longer. You see, I have bouts of sleepwalking. I don't recall these episodes but Richard has told me he has had to chase after me when I've walked out of the house in my nightgown.

"Two nights before Richard was murdered, I know I left the house because it had rained during the evening and my shoes were wet the next morning. I hadn't worn those shoes in weeks.

"I grew up on the wrong side of the tracks and knew some rather unsavory people. I ran into one of my old friends, Tony Horton, over a year ago. He knew I was married to Richard and knew Richard liked being seen with beautiful women. He gave me his business card and told me to call him if I ever decided to teach Richard a lesson. I found the card in the pocket of my jacket that morning too."

"Are you saying you think you hired a hit-man while you were asleep?"

"It's possible; whoever shot Richard was an expert marksman. Who else but a hired gun could have been that accurate at such a distance in a crowded theater?"

"Sophia, this sleep disorder; have you talked to a doctor about it?"

"Yes, and he said it's a result of too much stress and sleep deprivation. He gave me some medication to help with the stress, but it makes me feel groggy, so I don't take it."

"I don't know what to say. I don't know you well but I can't imagine you arranging for the murder of your husband or anyone else. Have you talked to this fellow, Tony, since Richard died?"

"No. I know I should call him but I'm afraid he'll tell me what I don't want to hear."

"Is there money missing from your bank account? I'm not familiar with what the going rate is for murder for hire, but I'd think it would make a noticeable dent in your finances."

"I never thought of that; I'll have to check for withdrawals. Unless Tony did it out of the kindness of his heart."

"I'm not an expert on hit-men either, but I doubt they'd commit murder as a favor."

"Samantha, thank you; you've made me feel better. Maybe I'm not responsible for Richard's death after all. I did love him, you know. I'm not oblivious to his imperfections, but I really did love him."

Samantha wondered what Sophia would have been like if she hadn't married Richard. It couldn't have been easy watching him parade around town with other women on his arm. She recalled the way he'd looked at her when she first met the man. The expression *undressing her with his eyes* came to mind. He really was a sleaze but he didn't deserve to die.

After an hour of pleasant conversation, the women parted. Sophia felt relaxed for the first time in years. She hadn't had a real friend since high school. Samantha told her to call anytime she was feeling stressed, maybe it would help if she talked it out and not keep it bottled up inside.

Samantha was driving back to her apartment and wondering if she should keep this information from Fletch. *There's really no reason to tell him about Sophia and her sleepwalking. It's absurd to think someone would hire a hit-man while asleep.* She was deep in thought and didn't notice the truck following behind her.

Inside that truck, Jimmy Lee took another swig of his beer to wash down the pills he had just swallowed.

Samantha pulled into her assigned spot in the parking garage of her apartment building. As she opened the car door and stepped out, a truck pulled behind her blocking her way. Her heart skipped a beat when Jimmy Lee Butler walked toward her. She opened her mouth to speak and saw the rifle in his hand. She turned to run and felt a severe pain at the back of her head before she fell to her knees and blacked out.

CHAPTER 12

"Fletch, this is Megan. I'm sorry to bother you, but have you heard from Samantha?"

"No, Megan, isn't she there with you at the apartment? I know she was headed that way after the funeral."

"She was here but she got a call and said she'd be out for an hour. That was three hours ago. I tried to call her on her cell phone, but it goes directly to voice mail. I'm worried, Fletch; it's not like Samantha to be out of touch for so long."

"I'll be right over. Do you know who she was meeting?"

"She didn't tell me; it might be my imagination but she seemed concerned when she left here."

*****

Fletch drove as fast as he could to Samantha's apartment building. He knew it was doubtful he'd get an answer, but he called her cell phone just the same. He parked in the visitor's parking lot and walked into the garage to see if her car happened to be there. He was relieved when he saw her VW in the usual spot, but panic set in when he discovered her purse on the floor beside the car. Her cell phone was in it along with her cash and credit cards eliminating a possible robbery. Fletch felt the hood of the car; it was cold. He looked through her purse and found a receipt for a purchase at the College Avenue Coffee Shop. The time stamp was almost three hours ago. *Who did she meet? Was she with that person now? It's obvious she didn't go willingly. Where could she be?* Fletch didn't often panic, but he was now and frighteningly so. He used the key Samantha had given him and walked into the lobby of the building. He didn't wait for the elevator, but took the stairs two at a time to the third floor. Mike was in the apartment with Megan.

"Has she called you?" asked Megan.

"No, her car's in the garage and this was on the floor," Fletch said, holding Samantha's purse in the air. "I'll check her calls to see who she was meeting."

Fletch went through the incoming calls until he came upon Sophia Delaney's name.

"That makes sense," said Megan. "I know Samantha talked with Mrs. Delaney at the reception after the funeral. She must have called her to continue their conversation. Samantha mentioned they were interrupted by Margaret Wakefield."

Fletch redialed Sophia's number.

"Samantha, I didn't expect to hear from you so soon."

"Mrs. Delaney, this is Detective Fletcher. I'm calling from Samantha's phone."

She told him about my sleepwalking, he's going to arrest me.

"Mrs. Delaney, are you there?"

"Yes, Detective, I'm here."

"Mrs. Delaney, I believe you met with Samantha earlier this afternoon, is that correct?"

"Yes, Detective, we did meet for coffee."

"Samantha is missing and I'm afraid she's been abducted. Her car's in the parking garage; her purse was beside it, but there's no sign of her. I believe you were the last person to see her."

"Samantha is missing? I can't believe it; we were together not two hours ago. Do you know who took her?"

"We don't have a clue. Is there anything you can think of that seemed unusual when you were with her?"

There was silence on the other end. Fletch assumed Mrs. Delaney was thinking.

"Yes. I don't know if it means anything, but I noticed a truck parked across the street from the coffee shop when I pulled my car into a spot in front. There was a young man with a ponytail in the driver's seat. I noticed him because he was staring at the coffee shop window. When we left, about an hour later, he was still there. When Samantha pulled away from the shop, he pulled away from the curb. You don't think he was the one who abducted her, do you?"

"Can you tell me anything about the truck? The color, the make, anything?"

"It was light, maybe tan or gray. It could have been a dirty white. I know nothing about makes and models of trucks, Detective. It was an older truck, not in the best of shape. I wish I could tell you more."

"You've been very helpful, Mrs. Delaney. I'll call you if I have any other questions."

"Please have Samantha call me as soon as she gets home; I'll worry until I hear from her."

Fletch ended the call and turned to Megan.

"What color is Jimmy's truck?" he asked.

"It's tan, a '99 Ranger. Why do you ask? Do you think Jimmy hurt Samantha?"

"He might have. Mrs. Delaney described a young guy with a ponytail. She knew he was in a light color truck but doesn't know the make or model."

"Oh, Fletch, it could be Jimmy. It's just like him to blame Samantha because I left. I'm so sorry I put her in danger. I should have known he'd do something to get revenge."

Fletch called the station requesting a search of Jimmy's apartment and an APB for Jimmy Lee Baker for questioning in the disappearance of Samantha Degan.

"Do you know of any place Jimmy would have taken her, Megan?"

"Is there a place called The Fort? I remember hearing Jimmy on the phone one time. He said he'd meet someone at The Fort. He didn't know I was listening and I didn't dare ask him what it was because I suspected it had something to do with drugs. I should have left him back then, but I didn't have the courage," she sobbed.

Mike held her in his arms. "This isn't your fault, Megan; it's Jimmy's fault and his alone. Stop beating yourself up."

Fletch knew it wasn't Megan's fault either but couldn't help but wish she'd never come into Samantha's life. He had to find her but had no idea where to look. He called his friend, Troy, who worked for the vice squad, asking if he'd ever heard of The Fort.

"It's probably a code for some meeting place. It could be any place on the Randolph Highway. There's a lot of drug activity out there in those abandon cabins near the river. I'd like to take a bulldozer and obliterate them all."

"Thanks, Troy. That's a big help."

Fletch headed for the door.

"What did he tell you, Fletch?" asked Mike.

"He had an idea where I can look."

"You aren't going alone?"

"Yes, I am. I can't wait for backup. I have to get to Samantha before that maniac hurts her."

"Call Robin, have her meet you there. In your state of mind, you might make the situation worse."

"You're probably right; I'll call her from the car."

*****

Samantha's head throbbed as she slowly opened her eyes. She had a difficult time focusing and didn't have any idea where she was. The last thing she remembered was seeing Jimmy Lee Baker with a rifle in his hand and then the pain and blackness. To the left was a small window. She could see the darkness in the sky. What had happened to her? Had she really been out for hours? It was eerily quiet in the room. Her hands were tied behind her with a heavy rope. She was seated in a straight back chair and her feet were secured to the bottom with another rope. She moved her feet and discovered the rope loosened. It was damp and musty in what looked to be a cabin. *I remember now. Jimmy Lee was in the parking garage. He had a rifle in his hand and he looked like a madman. I thought he was going to kill me. Where is he? Is he going to leave me here?*

The door opened and Samantha was looking into Jimmy Lee's eyes.

"So, you decided to wake up? It took you long enough. I thought you were going to die and take all the fun out of watching you suffer a slow death."

"Why do you want to kill me?" Samantha asked because she couldn't think of anything else to say.

"Why do I want to kill you? Because you don't deserve to live after you talked Megan into leaving me. Don't deny it, I know you and your stupid job is the reason she walked out. After I get rid of you, I'm going to go after her. I have plans for her. I might even let her live, but no man will ever want her after I get through with her."

Samantha felt a chill go up her spine. She guessed Jimmy was on drugs and didn't doubt he was capable of hurting her. He didn't notice that she was slowly loosening the rope around her feet until her legs were free.

"Jimmy, tell me one thing before I die. Did you kill Mayor Delaney?"

He laughed at her question.

"I should have. I should have killed him and Megan too, but I didn't do it. She told me it was part of the job. What kind of fool does she think I am? If someone hadn't put a bullet through his head, she would have slept with him that night. She'll pay for betraying me."

Jimmy walked toward her. He brought his fist back, but before he could hit her she raised both her legs and kicked him as hard as she could. He fell back in agony as Samantha ran out the opened door of the cabin. Her hands were still tied behind her back slowing her progress. She ran through the brush. Her legs were scratched and bleeding, but she didn't feel the pain. She finally made her way to the road and saw the lights of a truck barreling down the highway toward her. She heard the blast of the horn and could feel a shot of air as the truck barely missed her. She then heard a thump and a gunshot along with the squealing of the truck's brakes. She knew instantly that the truck had hit Jimmy but was unable to move.

The shaken truck driver opened the door to the cab.

"What's going on here?" he yelled.

He walked over to Jimmy's broken body. Samantha could hear him calling for Jimmy to wake up.

"Who's out there? I know someone's there. I didn't hit you, but I hit your friend."

Samantha walked across the road to the truck driver.

"Is he dead?" she asked.

"I don't think so. What is this game you're playing? You both could have been killed."

He looked at Samantha and saw her hands tied behind her back.

"Are you all right, miss? Did this guy hurt you?"

"He was about to, but thank God you came along when you did. Would you mind calling Detective Fletcher? I'll give you his number."

"Let's get you out of these ropes and you can call him yourself."

After she was free and on her phone, she said, "Fletch, it's me. I'm sorry I missed our dinner date." She turned the phone over to the truck driver who gave Fletch their location and asked him to send an ambulance.

"I'm not sure this guy is worth saving, but I suppose that isn't my decision to make."

*****

Fletch arrived in less than five minutes. He held Samantha gently in his arms. She had dried blood on the back of her head, her legs were scratched and bleeding, and she had rope burns on her wrists.

"I'm fine, Fletch. I'm not sure about Jimmy, though; you might want to see to him."

"I don't care about Jimmy's condition after what he did to you."

The ambulance arrived and the paramedics put Jimmy on a stretcher and hauled him away. Samantha said she was fine, but Fletch insisted she be seen in the emergency room before going home.

After giving his insurance information and signing a police report, the truck driver was sent on his way to deliver the goods he was transporting. Samantha thanked him again and, to his delight, gave him a hug.

Samantha had a slight concussion from the gun barrel hitting her in the head. She was told to take it easy for the next few days.

Jimmy Lee had a broken arm and leg from being hit by the truck. The more serious damage was done by his gun that had discharged when he was hit. A bullet was lodged in his spine and it was doubtful he'd ever walk again. He was arrested for kidnapping and, eventually, for drug trafficking. Megan attempted to visit him in the hospital and he refused to see her. He blamed her for everything bad that ever happened to him.

CHAPTER 13

Samantha's run-in with Jimmy Lee was nothing more than an unpleasant memory. She felt relief that he was safely locked away, waiting to be sentenced for his various crimes. Fletch told her he pled guilty to the charge of kidnapping and agreed to testify for the prosecution against his cohorts about the drug activity. He was despondent over his paralysis and didn't care whether there was retaliation or not.

Although Megan wasn't able to totally erase the memory of Jimmy from her mind, she was happier than she'd ever been. Looking back on her time with him, she could see how he had controlled her. Samantha could see the change in Megan and it helped that she and Mike Thompson were becoming very good friends. Mike knew friendship was what Megan needed now. In time, he thought she might be willing to give more and he would be a willing recipient.

*****

"Fletch, the Commissioner is on the phone," said Robin Wells. "He wants to know what's taking so long solving the Richard Delaney murder. Mayor Wakefield is badgering him, or so he says."

"Tell him it's taking so long because we don't have a clue who did it. No, don't tell him that. I'll talk to him."

Fletch forced a smile on his face before he spoke.

"Hello, Commissioner. What can I do for you?"

"Fletch, I'm getting pressure on this Delaney murder. What's the hold-up, son? You were two seats away from the mayor when he was shot. I'm beginning to question your competence. What about that drug dealer who kidnapped your girlfriend? Can you pin it on him?"

"I wish it was that easy, but the evidence doesn't point to him. My guess is it was a professional job and won't be easy to solve."

"Your guess isn't good enough. I want you and Wells to work on this case exclusively. When's that baby due? Tell her the timing isn't very convenient. I wish she'd talked to me before she got herself knocked up again. Pregnancy is one of the many reasons not to have women on the force."

"I'll be sure to pass that along to Wells, sir. If there's nothing else, I'll get to work solving the murder."

Fletch's phone was on speaker and Robin was listening to the conversation.

"Did you hear that, Wells? The Commissioner wants to know when you get horny again?" Fletch laughed.

"A new form of birth control. I'll just picture the Commissioner's face. What a mood killer that would be."

Suddenly, Robin stood up quickly, grimaced and doubled over in pain. "Please call Frank. I'd better get to the hospital. I think I'm in labor. I'll have one of the patrolmen drive me."

"No, you won't. I'll drive you."

Fletch had delivered his share of babies, but preferred they were born in a hospital with a doctor present. He placed the portable flasher on his car and drove quickly but carefully to the emergency entrance of Lancashire hospital.

Frank, who worked less than a mile from the hospital, was waiting for Robin when she arrived. Although this was their third child, Frank worried about his wife. This pregnancy hadn't been easy on her. He wondered if it was a wise decision to have another child but it was a little late to reconsider now.

Robin smiled at her husband. "This one is really anxious to meet us," she said as a pain took her breath away.

She was transported to labor and delivery where she gave birth to a healthy baby girl within minutes.

Soon thereafter, Fletch checked in on his partner who had never looked so happy. He told her little Emma was beautiful although he didn't think newborn babies were the best-looking creatures.

On his way back to the station, he called Samantha to give her the news. Because everything had happened so quickly, it was the first chance he'd had to tell her about Robin and the baby.

He became alarmed when she didn't answer her phone. Ever since her ordeal with Jimmy, Fletch was constantly worried about her. He was happy her book was such a success, but too much notoriety could bring danger too. His next call was to Megan.

"Megan, it's Fletch. I'm sorry to bother you, but Samantha isn't picking up her phone. Is she there?"

"No, Fletch, she was meeting Mayor Wakefield's executive assistant, Wanda Anderson. She probably turned her phone off. She said Wanda had some information about Richard Delaney's murder."

*****

An hour earlier, Samantha sat at her desk finishing, what she hoped would be, the last rewrite on her mystery novel. She was nervous about the book. *Memoirs of Professor Stonehill* had been a success, but the subject matter was different from a fictional murder mystery.

Maybe she chose the wrong career. The world was filled with novelists, and very few could make a living writing.

It surprised her that there was interest in having her speak at various functions in the area. She was also surprised that public speaking brought her pleasure. She wished Professor Stonehill was still alive and could know he was still influencing people. Samantha was glad she was a fastidious note taker and had jotted down so many of the professor's clever anecdotes and heartwarming stories.

The ringing of her cell phone startled her.

"Ms. Degan, Wanda Anderson calling. I'm executive assistant to Mayor Forrest Wakefield."

"Hello, Ms. Anderson. I believe we met at Mayor Delaney's funeral. How many I help you?"

"I might be able to help you. I know you're looking into the murder of Richard Delaney. Your beau, Detective Fletcher, asked me to call if I had any information for him. I'm afraid I don't have anything concrete, and I don't want to be on the record. I thought if I talked to you, it would be off the record."

"Ms. Anderson, I would be happy to meet with you. However, if you do have information that will solve the mayor's murder, I must pass it along to the authorities."

"I understand. I know who killed the former mayor, but I don't have any evidence."

"I'd like to meet with you. I can come to the mayor's office or I'll meet you at a coffee shop or restaurant."

"I'd prefer to meet you here if it's convenient for you. Mayor Wakefield will be out of the office all day."

"I'll be there in ten minutes."

*****

It struck Samantha that Wanda Anderson looked older than her voice suggested. With her mousy brown hair wrapped in a bun at the back of her neck and her unbecoming polyester pantsuit, she looked well past retirement age. Samantha couldn't help but think of the stylish Margaret Wakefield. Wanda was no competition for her employer's wife.

"Ms. Degan, thank you for coming."

"Please call me Samantha. May I call you Wanda?"

"I suppose that will be appropriate because of the nature of what I'm about to tell you," she whispered so quietly that Samantha barely made out what was being said.

Wanda closed the door to her office. Calling the front desk, she told the receptionist she didn't wish to be disturbed.

"I don't know how to say this other than to come right out with it. Cindy Matthews murdered her boss. I don't know if she killed him herself or hired someone to do it for her, but I'm sure she did it."

Samantha had only spoken with Cindy the day of the funeral and didn't know her well, but the girl didn't strike her as someone capable of murder. Cindy had been a comfort to Megan when the media badgered her after the mayor's death.

"What makes you think Mayor Delaney's assistant was responsible for his death, Wanda?"

"She was in love with him, you know. Cindy loved her boss. When she started to work for him, he took her to all the social functions he should have attended with his wife. I know he was bedding her; it was disgusting. She pranced around these offices with her nose in the air. She thought she was something special, but she was nothing but a common trollop. She had no respect for these dignified offices. Mayor Delaney became bored with her and began choosing others to take her place. She wasn't so high and mighty after that. Mayor Wakefield got rid of her after he took over. There was no need to have her kind around anymore."

"Are you saying Cindy Matthews killed Mayor Delaney because he ended their affair?"

"Not only that, everyone knew Richard was going to be running for governor. Well, I happened to be in the ladies room when I heard Cindy telling Mindy Bellows that Richard was looking for someone more sophisticated to be his executive assistant when he was elected governor. You should have heard her, she was fit to be tied."

The look of satisfaction on Wanda's face didn't go unnoticed by Samantha.

"Did you hear her say anything that indicated she planned to kill the mayor?"

"No, but I'm sure she was thinking about it."

"I'd like to talk to Cindy. I don't suppose you have a phone number for her."

"I'll get it for you."

"How long have you worked for Mayor Wakefield, Wanda?"

"I've been his right hand for over twenty-two years. He's a brilliant man. Unfortunately, he hadn't reached his full potential until he took over as mayor."

"Richard Delaney's death wasn't totally in vain then," Samantha said sarcastically.

"I should say not. Some of us didn't mourn him at all."

Wanda Anderson is a piece of work. I would love to know what she thinks of Mrs. Wakefield, Samantha thought as she walked out of the city government offices, holding a slip of paper with Cindy Matthew's address and phone number on it.

Samantha called Cindy from her car. Cindy answered immediately and agreed to talk with Samantha, inviting her to her apartment.

Cindy lived in a Victorian-style home that had been converted into three apartments. The tree-lined street was inviting with old-fashioned street lamps and colorful flowers along the median. The home was a soft red brick with turrets and dormers on the three-story building. The porch that encircled the front door was welcoming.

Samantha rang the doorbell and was greeted by a smiling Cindy Matthews.

"Hello, Samantha. It's nice seeing you again. I'm afraid I made a terrible fool of myself when we last met."

"You didn't make a fool of yourself; you were understandably upset."

Samantha's first impression of Cindy held true. She was far from being a trollop, as Wanda had put it. She was dressed modestly in a V-neck, short-sleeved cotton top and lightweight capris.

"Please come in; my apartment is on the second floor."

Samantha followed Cindy up the winding staircase to her apartment. She opened the door and Samantha almost gasped.

"Cindy, this is lovely," she said as she looked around the large living area. Three floor to ceiling rounded windows overlooked the street below and a park on the right. Cindy had furnished the room in pastels with a white sofa and soft pink chairs. The walls were painted lavender with white trim. The kitchen appliances and cupboards were white, the walls were a soft lemon color with windows looking out to the river.

"I do love it here; I just don't know how much longer I'll be able to keep up with the rent. I haven't had luck finding a job since I left the mayor's office. I'm guessing you got my phone number and address from Wanda Anderson."

"Yes, she did give it to me."

"She probably told you I killed Richard too. The old bat never did like me, but it surprised me when she accused me of murder."

"She accused you?"

"Yes, she's convinced I killed him because he broke my heart. That part is true. I'm ashamed of it, but I thought I was in love with Richard. She's also convinced we were having an affair, and that part isn't true. I was willing; it was Richard who remained faithful to his wife."

"You accompanied him to several events."

"I did until people started talking. He thought it looked better if he had a variety of women on his arm. He was a chronic flirt; I honestly believe he never did more than flirt. He had a tremendous ego and he liked making people think he was a stud. It's only been a matter of weeks since his death, but I've psychoanalyzed myself and I think I'm finally getting over him.

"When he said I wasn't suitable for the job of assistant to the governor, I wanted him dead. I pictured myself walking into his office and stabbing him in his heart. I even thought of poisoning him. That's when I decided I'd gone off the deep end. I made an appointment with a psychiatrist, but canceled it when Richard died. I do have an alibi for that night. I was at a birthday celebration for my three-year-old niece. Almost all my relatives were there too."

"I'm not accusing you of murder, but I must tell you, the police are looking into the possibility of this being a professional job."

"Well, I guess I'm not off the hook then, but I wouldn't know where to find a hit-man, but I suppose I could if I tried."

"You've been very honest with me about your feelings for Mayor Delaney. I don't think you would be so candid if you were hiding a murder."

"Thank you for saying that. I think I'll call Wanda and assure her she has nothing to fear from me. I don't have any intention of taking her job from her."

"She didn't strike me as the insecure type, but you know her better than I do. By the way, do you remember Megan Fairbanks? She's working for me now."

"Yes, of course, I remember her. She's a nice girl. I didn't care for her boyfriend. I can't remember his name, but he was a mean character."

"He's out of the picture now."

"Good! Please give Megan my best."

CHAPTER 14

How interesting, Samantha thought. *Mayor Richard Delaney affected different people in different ways. She had him pegged when she'd first met him and figured out immediately that he was a shameless flirt.*

Upon returning to the apartment, Megan met her at the door.

"Fletch is trying to reach you. Your phone must be turned off. You'd better call him right away; he's worried about you."

"I did turn it off and forgot about it. I'll call him; it's nice having someone worry about me."

"You're a lucky woman; I don't know why you're hesitating about accepting his marriage proposal. Don't let one of the good guys get away."

Samantha rolled her eyes at her friend. Megan was right about Fletch being one of the good guys. She didn't want to burden him with a wife who had one successful book and might never have another published in her lifetime. After so many rewrites, she was beginning to think maybe her desire to be a writer was a pipe-dream.

Fletch picked up on the first ring.

"Samantha, are you all right? After what happened with Jimmy Lee Butler, I get nervous when I can't reach you."

"I'm sorry, Fletch; I'll keep my phone on vibrate from now on. Thanks for worrying about me."

"You didn't ask why I was trying to get in touch with you. Robin had a baby girl this afternoon. She and Emma are doing well."

"Fletch, that's wonderful! I'll bet she's a beautiful baby."

"Robin seems to think so; personally, I think she looks a little like a prune."

"Don't say that; the poor little girl has been through an ordeal simply being born. I'd love to see her."

"I'm just getting ready to leave the office. Why don't I swing by and pick you up? We can go to the hospital together. Frank was going to bring the boys in to meet their sister. What's a couple more visitors?"

"I'll be waiting. I had a couple of interesting conversations today and want to tell you about them. I'm afraid it has nothing to do with solving the mayor's murder other than eliminating possible suspects."

*****

Samantha was excited about seeing Emma. She hadn't been around a newborn baby since she was a teenager. Two of her older brothers were married by then and each had a child of their own. Samantha smiled remembering the day her first nephew, Matthew, had been born. She was in awe of his tiny fingers and toes. It was hard to believe that big strapping adolescent was ever so small. Since moving to Lancashire to attend school, she only saw her nieces and nephews when visiting her folks.

*****

Fletch pulled up in front of the apartment building where Samantha was waiting for him.

"Am I late?" he asked.

"Not at all; I just now came downstairs. I can't wait to see the baby. Did Robin go into labor at the office? I know she was scheduled to work today."

"She did work and went into labor in my office. Emma didn't waste any time getting here. Luckily, we made it to the hospital just in time."

On the drive to the hospital, Samantha told Fletch about the phone call she'd received from Wanda Anderson.

"She's a mousy little thing, and I'd guess she's had a secret crush on Forrest Wakefield for years."

"I wonder if Madam First Lady knows that?"

"She probably doesn't care. If she felt threatened by the competition, I'm sure Wanda would have been long gone by now."

"You mean permanently gone like Richard Delaney? Do you think that woman's ambition for her husband could have been taken to such an extreme level?"

"The thought has crossed my mind, but murder to further her husband's career seems a bit drastic. My gut feeling is this was a spontaneous crime of passion and not a calculated murder plot requiring a hired gun."

"You're sounding like a cop. Have you ever thought of applying to the police academy?"

"If my mystery novel bombs, I might do that," Samantha laughed.

*****

They arrived at the hospital and walked directly to Robin's room.

The Wells' family made a beautiful picture—Robin holding Emma, Frank with his arm around his wife and the two boys looking in awe at their little sister.

The scene brought tears to Samantha's eyes. She looked closely at the baby. Emma didn't look at all like a prune. She was beautiful, her eyes were open and she appeared to be looking directly at Samantha.

Robin looked relaxed and happy. Fletch couldn't believe this was the same woman who was writhing in pain a few hours ago.

"You look terrific, Robin. You're good at this mother thing."

"I'm not sure how good I am. I fell asleep two minutes after you left and I just woke up. I'm sure Emma thinks her mama is a wimp."

Frank and Fletch took the boys to the cafeteria and left the women alone to talk.

Robin handed Emma to Samantha. She felt nervous about holding such a tiny baby, but it seemed natural.

"Emma likes you, Samantha. I can hear her asking you when you're going to marry Fletch and have a baby of your own."

Samantha laughed. "Did you really say that, Emma? Your voice sounded just like your mother's."

Samantha was still holding Emma when Fletch and the others returned to the room. He never considered himself a sentimental guy, but he liked the sight of Samantha with a baby in her arms.

"We should let you have some family time. Thank you for letting me hold Emma; she's precious."

"I'll be using every day allowed for maternity leave, but don't be strangers. We'll have you over for dinner again very soon."

"We'll come, but we'll bring the dinner," said Fletch. "Benivitto's has great takeout."

"That sounds wonderful."

*****

"Robin looks great and Emma doesn't look anything like a prune."

"No, she's improved since I first saw her."

They walked out to the parking lot. Fletch held the door open for her.

"Yes," Samantha said.

"Yes? Yes, what?"

"Yes, I'll marry you."

"What?"

"I said yes, I'll marry you, that is, if the offer is still on the table."

"Oh, baby, are you serious? When? Tomorrow can't be soon enough."

"Mom will never forgive me if we aren't married in Ashville."

"How long will that take? When my sister was married, it was months in the planning stages."

"Not that long. My mother knows I'm not in favor of big, expensive weddings. I'd like to be married in the chapel in Wedgwood Park. It's a beautiful little church and I do mean little. I hope your parents will be able to make the trip."

"My folks will be there, they never thought I'd find a girl like you. I know that's so because Mom told me that the last time I talked to her; you made an impression on her and Dad when they visited last month."

"My family likes you too; the fact that you carry a gun probably influenced my overprotective brothers."

"What made you change your mind about marrying me?"

"I always wanted to marry you, I just didn't want to come into the marriage without a job or any sign that I would be a success as an author. I think when you said I could join the police force it made me realize there are other things in life I can do besides writing. Megan told me I should snap you up before someone else does. Watching Robin and her family made me realize that this is the life I want no matter what profession I choose."

"The timing is perfect. I've tried to think of a way to tell you this without sounding like I was pressuring you to get married. There's a house in Robin's neighborhood that's for sale. I have an appointment to see it tonight at seven o'clock. Lately, I've thought that a house would be a good investment. I've been paying rent for several years now and have nothing to show for it. I'd hoped you would go with me to see it."

"I'd love to. That's a beautiful area."

Fletch looked at his watch, "We don't have time for more than a hamburger. This isn't the way I expected to celebrate our engagement."

"We never do anything in a conventional way. Remember how we met?"

*****

Fletch drove to Brookside Burgers where they sat outside enjoying the fresh air and the sound of water softly hitting the boulders as it flowed by.

They ordered their meals and while they waited, Fletch took hold of her hand. Samantha was looking into his eyes and didn't realize, for a moment, that he was slipping a ring on her finger.

She looked down at a sparkling white gold ring with a diamond in the center and enhanced by more diamonds lining the band.

"Fletch, this is the most beautiful ring I've ever seen. I love it. How did you know I was going to come to my senses and agree to marry you today?"

"It's been in my pocket for months. I always hoped you would agree to marry me and I wanted to be ready. I pictured us being in a little classier setting than this."

"Are you kidding? It's beautiful here. Listen to the babbling brook and the singing of birds; it's a perfect way to start our lives together."

Fletch smiled as he thought of Rachel. She wouldn't have heard the water or the birds, she only wanted the glitz and glamor that money could bring. He said a silent prayer of gratitude that she'd dumped him for a man who could give her all the luxuries she wanted. He looked up and watched as Samantha stood and walked over to him planting a kiss on his lips.

The other diners began to clap for the couple. Samantha held her hand in the air and shouted more loudly than she'd intended, "We're engaged!"

Several of the women approached their table to admire her new ring that fit perfectly on her finger.

"When's the wedding?" someone asked.

"As soon as possible," said Fletch. "I don't want to risk the bride changing her mind."

"Not a chance," replied Samantha as the waitress arrived with their burgers and fries.

*****

Samantha was still admiring her ring when Fletch pulled in front of the house. It was far from the starter home Samantha had envisioned. The exterior was brick with light gray siding and inviting traditional grill patterned windows trimmed in white. Tall trees towered over the back of the house with two shade trees in the front yard. Low growing shrubs lined the walkway leading to the large front porch.

The real estate agent, Ginny Slade, met them at the door and introduced herself to Samantha.

"The owners have been transferred to the Midwest and are anxious to sell. As I told you on the phone, Detective Fletcher, I think we can get a good price on the property."

Samantha tried to keep the excitement out of her voice as she examined every inch of the house.

"Fletch, this house has four bedrooms; do you think we'll need that many?" she looked at him skeptically.

"Twins run in my family," he laughed. "It seems like a lot, but we can use one as your office and another as mine. That only leaves one bedroom to fill. Maybe four bedrooms won't be enough after all."

She gave him a friendly punch on the arm. "I love it but can we afford it? My book is selling now but we don't know when that well will run dry."

"You forget that until I met you I lived like a monk. I've been able to save enough money to make a sizable down payment that will bring the monthly mortgage to a reasonable level. I want you to concentrate on your writing and not worry about finances. I think I'm capable of supporting both of us and six or seven children in the future." He winked at her.

"Nobody has six or seven children these days; how about one or two?"

"It's a start. Do you want to look at more places?"

"I'll be happy to look, but I know I'll come back to this one. I've already decided on where the Christmas tree will stand in the family room."

"You do plan ahead, don't you?"

Fletch told Ginny to make an offer on the home.

CHAPTER 15

Samantha woke up the next morning to the smell of coffee and bacon. She was going to weigh two hundred pounds if Fletch continued to make breakfast for her after they were married. She looked at her ring for the thousandth time since the moment he'd slipped it on her finger. Yesterday had been a day to remember; she was engaged and had helped choose the house she and Fletch would be sharing as husband and wife. There were so many things to do. First, she would call her parents. She would ask her mother to find out when the chapel in Wedgwood Park would be available. The sooner the better. Now that she and Fletch were engaged, she didn't want to wait to be his wife.

"Good morning, husband-to-be. It smells wonderful in here."

"I know you want me to cut down on the bacon, but we're celebrating this morning. I had a call from Ginny; the owners of the house accepted our offer. She's going to work out the details and get back to me. Congratulations, homeowner!"

"Oh, Fletch, I couldn't be happier. I don't know why I didn't say yes to you months ago."

"I don't know why either; I'm quite a catch, you know."

"I know. I'd better call my mother before she and Dad go off to play a round of golf."

"I think our parents will get along well; mine like golf too."

"You were going to tell me about your conversations with Wanda Anderson and Cindy Matthews, but we had other things on our mind last night." He winked.

"Those two are as different as night and day. Wanda is an insecure, vindictive woman who insists Cindy Matthews killed Richard Delaney because he was going to replace her as his executive assistant. I called Cindy to set up a meeting. She invited me to stop by and couldn't have been more gracious. She admitted she had thoughts of murdering him after he told her he wouldn't need her services when he became governor. She thought she loved him, but nothing ever happened between them. I believe her and I don't think she killed him or arranged to have him killed."

"His Honor was a real gem, wasn't he? This case has me baffled. There are several suspects and it doesn't look like any of them have the stomach for murder. What about Wanda Anderson? Do you think she was trying to divert your attention away from her as the murderer?"

"I got the feeling from the woman that, if she'd killed Richard, she would be bragging about it to the world. She practically said she'd do anything for her boss."

"Forrest Wakefield has my sincere sympathy; I don't know how he deals with his snob of a wife and his ill-tempered executive assistant."

"I'd better get to the station; the work will be piling up without Robin. They're sending a rookie over to help out this afternoon. The last time Robin had a kid I was stuck with some knucklehead who didn't know what he was doing."

"Maybe you should tell Robin how much you miss her when she isn't there."

"What? And give her a swelled head?" Fletch laughed as he kissed Samantha goodbye.

*****

It was too early to call Sophia but she did want to speak to her. She'd read in the local paper that the presentation of *The Music Man* had received rave reviews. No mention was made of the murder that took place that night.

Megan came bouncing through the door. Samantha couldn't believe the change in her since Jimmy Lee Butler was no longer in her life.

"Good morning, Samantha; isn't it a beautiful day?"

"It looks beautiful, I haven't been outside yet. Your face is flushed; are you all right?"

"I've never been better. Mike stopped by earlier and asked me to have breakfast with him at Rudy's. We sat outside on the patio; it's so pretty with the fountains and ponds. The birds were singing in the trees. Mike says that's his favorite place during the summer and asked me to have dinner with him."

"I hope he's not rushing you. It wasn't that long ago that you were planning your life with Jimmy in it."

"I think I always knew it wasn't going to work out with Jimmy. I'm sorry he's in trouble and that he's paralyzed, but I refuse to feel guilty about his circumstances. He brought everything on himself."

"I just don't want Mike to be hurt; he's a good guy and a good friend."

"Samantha, I won't hurt him. I promise."

"It's really none of my business. I want both of you to be happy. If you can be happy together, that's even better."

"Samantha!" Megan shouted. "Your ring! Fletch gave you a ring! Does that mean a wedding soon?"

Megan examined the ring, sparkling as the sun hit it.

"It's beautiful," she cried. "You and Fletch are perfect for each other. Will he be moving in here? Will I be in the way? When's the wedding?"

"No, you won't be in the way. I'll be giving up the apartment when the lease runs out, but in the meantime, we'll continue to work out of here. Fletch and I are buying a house. There will be plenty of room for an office there. It's not too far from here, so it will be a short drive for you. The wedding will be in Ashville as soon as possible. I don't want to wait any longer to start my life with Fletch."

*****

The morning progressed quickly. Fletch called to say he missed his soon-to-be wife. After a forty-five-minute discussion with her mom and dad telling them the news of her engagement, her mother called another five times to make plans for the wedding. Samantha didn't mind the interruptions; she knew her mother was excited that her daughter was ready to settle down. The principal of Lancashire High School called to ask if she'd consider teaching a writing class. Samantha promised to give it serious consideration. Her agent called to say her mystery was on its way to the publishers and to arrange times for book signings.

Samantha's head was spinning when her cell phone rang.

"Samantha, it's Sophia Delaney. Did I catch you at a bad time?"

"No, Sophia," she lied. "What's up?"

"If you aren't busy, I thought you might like to stop by for lunch. Eloise is out for the day and I thought we could have a nice visit. I so enjoy your company."

Samantha had planned to work through the lunch hour but sensed Sophia needed a friend to talk to.

"That would be lovely, Sophia. I'll see you at twelve thirty."

*****

Samantha drove out of the parking garage into the bright sunshine. Megan was right; it was a beautiful day. She turned off the air conditioning and rolled down the windows to let in the fresh air.

The home Sophia shared with Richard was exquisite. It wasn't nearly as large as Stonehill Manor where she'd worked for Professor Stonehill, but still very impressive with its white pillars and fountain in the center of the perfectly manicured lawn. It hadn't occurred to Samantha before, but this home was a smaller version of The White House in Washington, DC.

Sophia greeted her at the door.

"Come in, Samantha. Thank you for accepting my invitation. I so enjoyed our talk the other day and hope I'm not imposing on you."

"Don't be silly, I'm happy to be here."

"I thought we could dine out back by the pool; it's such a beautiful day."

*****

The two women talked like old friends. Sophia noticed Samantha's ring and was happy to hear of the upcoming marriage. Samantha mentioned the article she'd read praising Sophia's performance in *The Music Man.* The production was still being played in several cities near Lancashire with Sophia's understudy playing Marian.

"Maybe you should try again; you were so good in the part."

"I'd like to, but I'm not sleeping well and I'm not sure I have the energy for it."

"Are you still sleepwalking?"

"I don't know; the nightmares are so bad, I never know what's real and what isn't. I keep dreaming of being in the theater and seeing a man with a black hood over his head. He points a gun at Richard and slowly pulls the trigger. I try to tell him to stop, but I don't have any voice and my feet won't move. Richard falls over and I scream. That's when the man lifts off his hood and it's Tony Horton telling me he did what I'd asked. I hate going to bed at night. If it weren't for the pills, I'd probably never fall asleep at all."

"What kind of pills are you taking? Are they prescribed by a doctor?"

"Oh no, nothing like that! They're an herbal supplement. Eloise gave me some months ago when I couldn't fall asleep. They are wonderfully soothing."

Samantha had read articles in magazines about the danger of some herbal medications. She didn't want to pressure Sophia, but she did want to know more about the pills.

"Sophia, what's the name of this medication?"

"Do you need something to help you sleep? I'm sure you have a lot on your mind with all that's going on in your life. I make sure I have an ample supply; I'll give you a bottle to try."

Sophia disappeared into the house and returned with a bottle marked Valerian Root, an herbal supplement. Samantha thanked her for them and put the bottle in her purse.

*****

After Samantha left the Delaney home, she called Fletch at the station.

"I'd like to stop by if you have a minute to see me."

"It sounds serious. Does it have anything to do with your visit to Sophia?"

"I don't know; I'll be there in ten minutes. I need your advice about something."

*****

Samantha always got a chill up her spine when she walked into the police station. The memory of the time Professor Stonehill was murdered and she was arrested came back to her. She shook off the feeling and secured her visitor's pass from the front desk. The entire staff knew her and knew of her relationship with Fletch. Even the surliest of officers greeted her with a friendly smile.

"What's up, beautiful? You sounded worried on the phone."

"It's Sophia; she's having nightmares about Richard's murder. She's afraid she hired someone to kill him while she was sleepwalking. She mentioned these pills and gave me some, thinking I needed them. They're supposed to help with falling asleep, but I thought you might be able to help me find out if they can be harmful."

"I'll call Dr. Melville; he should be able to tell me if there's anything wrong with these things. They look harmless, but we can have the lab check them out too."

"I knew you'd be able to help me. I worry about Sophia; she's at the breaking point. Have you noticed their home looks like a replica of The White House? I asked Sophia about it and she told me it was custom-built for Richard. He really thought a lot of himself, didn't he?"

CHAPTER 16

"Your mother called. Your phone keeps going to voicemail and she wanted you to call her as soon as you get in. Samantha, your mom sounds so nice. She invited me to the wedding."

"I hope you'll come. I'll have to make sure Mike gets an invitation too."

*****

Samantha called her mother. She knew she could count on her mother to arrange everything the way she wanted. The chapel in Wedgwood Park had been reserved and Reverend Bennett said he would be delighted to marry them. A room at the Ashville Hilton was reserved and would be catered by Alfred Greenfield Catering. Alfred was a school friend of Samantha's oldest brother and the best caterer in town.

"Mom, I knew you could do it, but I never expected you'd have everything taken care of so quickly."

"This is only the beginning. I've waited a long time for my only daughter to marry. I have all sorts of ideas."

"Just remember to keep it simple," Samantha pleaded, knowing it wouldn't do any good.

*****

"Hi, sweetheart," Fletch said, laughing. "I just got off the phone with my mother. She and Dad are driving to Ashville tomorrow to meet with your folks and discuss the wedding. Are you sure you don't want to run off to Las Vegas? This thing is getting complicated."

"Let's let them do their thing; your mother called me too. She's as excited as my mother about this. I told Mom we wanted it simple, but I think that fell on deaf ears."

"In between my mother's phone calls, I heard from Doc Melville. Valerian Root is from the Valerian plant, whatever that is. It's used for relief of anxiety and as a sleeping aid. Doc doesn't recommend it for his patients because of possible side effects, including liver damage. The drug has also been known to cause vivid nightmares in some people.

"I had the lab check out the pills you gave me. They're exactly what it says on the bottle—nothing has been added to them."

"I wonder how I can convince Sophia to stop taking them; she seems to think they're a miracle drug."

"Maybe you could talk to Eloise. She acts like her guardian."

"Eloise is the one who gave them to her; she probably takes them herself and they don't affect her like they do Sophia."

"I can give you Doc Melville's number if you'd like to pass it along to Sophia."

"I know she has her own doctor, but I don't know if she's talked to him about these pills. I guess I'm going to have to pay her another visit. I hope Eloise isn't there. I'd rather talk to Sophia alone."

"Good luck. I'll see you around six o'clock."

"I'll be here."

*****

Sophia was surprised to hear from Samantha again so soon.

"Sophia, I have something to discuss with you. Would it be all right if I stopped by for a little while?"

"Of course, is something wrong, Samantha?"

"No, nothing's wrong. I just wanted to talk to you about the possible cause of your nightmares."

*****

Sophia was waiting at the door when Samantha arrived.

"Sophia, how much do you know about these pills you're taking?" She held up the bottle of Valerian Root.

"What's to know? They help me fall asleep. Is there something else I should know?"

"Have you told your doctor you're taking these?"

"No, they aren't real medication. It never occurred to me to tell him."

"Doctor Delmar Melville works closely with the police department. He told Fletch that Valerian Root can cause vivid nightmares in some people. Do you remember if your nightmares started after you began taking these pills?"

"I don't remember. I've been taking them for a couple of years. I was having trouble sleeping and Eloise suggested them. She takes them herself and has never mentioned nightmares."

"They don't affect everyone the same way. Would you be willing to stop taking them for a while to see if the nightmares go away?"

"You don't understand; without my pills, I can't sleep. I won't give them up. It's not like I'm using heroin or cocaine. These little pills are from a plant. What harm could they do?"

"Cocaine and heroin come from plants too."

"Samantha, I thought you were my friend. I need my pills. I don't want to talk about it anymore."

"I'm not going to pressure you, Sophia. I'm sure it's not pleasant being unable to fall asleep. You could try playing soft music to help you relax. You told me you used to do yoga exercises every day. Maybe you could start those again. I care about you, Sophia, I don't know if those pills are causing the nightmares, but if there's a chance you can have a peaceful night's sleep, isn't it worth trying?"

"I'll think about it," said Sophia. "That's all I can tell you."

*****

Sophia did think about Samantha's words. She picked up her iPad and began a search for her precious Valerian Root pills. She discovered that there was significant evidence that the pills were causing the nightmares. Would she be able to give them up and still sleep at night? It had been a while since she'd done yoga exercises, but some of the poses came back to her.

She found her old yoga mat in the back of the closet and began some of the routines she remembered.

Eloise returned to the house and smiled as she watched Sophia in a downward dog pose. Eloise envied the tiny waist and slim hips of the younger woman.

"I'm glad to see you're getting back into a routine," Eloise said.

"It feels good. I'd forgotten how relaxing yoga can be; you should try it, Eloise."

"Believe me, even if I could maneuver my body into that position, you don't want to see my tush in the air. I stopped by to check on you before I go home."

"You don't have to worry about me. I'll be fine."

Eloise did worry. She worried about Sophia and mostly she worried about what she would do without a job now that Richard was gone. She had spent the last five years taking care of the Delaneys.

She loved being Richard's campaign manager. He had nothing going for him except his good looks and she had turned him into a winning candidate.

She'd thought about approaching Forrest Wakefield about working as his campaign manager for the next election, but she wouldn't be able to tolerate Mrs.

Wakefield. *Everything was going so well, why did it have to change?* Eloise thought to herself while driving home from the Delaney house.

*****

"You sound distracted; are you all right?" asked Fletch when he called later that afternoon.

"I'm not distracted. I'm driving home from my visit with Sophia. I'm not too far from the station. How close are you to stopping for the day?"

"I'm ready to leave and meet my wife-to-be. Have you heard from the folks today?"

"Only a half-dozen times. You'd think it was William and Kate getting married all over again."

"My Mom called me twice; your parents are my parents' new best friends," said Fletch

"That's good; they can keep each other occupied. Do you want to meet somewhere for dinner?"

"Why don't we call for takeout; I'd love to spend the evening alone with you."

"Sounds good. Will you look up a name for me before you leave?" asked Samantha. "See what you can find out about a guy named Tony Horton. I think he's from the west side of Lancashire but that was a few years ago."

"I'll see what I can find. Drive safely and I'll see you shortly."

Sophia is convinced she met with this Tony guy. She mentioned the possibility of a split personality. Could it be true? thought Samantha. *I hope I didn't go too far in telling her how dangerous that herbal supplement can be. I think she was beginning to trust me and I don't want to ruin the relationship.*

*****

"Hi, sweetheart; it's me," Fletch said when he called her back in record time. "Tony Horton was killed in a drive-by shooting three months ago. He was walking out of a convenience store he'd just held up when someone took a shot at him and killed him instantly. He had an extensive criminal record. Why did you want to know about him?"

"I'll tell you all about it when you get to the apartment. Hurry, I miss you."

CHAPTER 17

Sophia's bedroom began to fill with sunlight. Her first thought was that she didn't sleep a wink. She'd taken Samantha's advice and did some sleep-inducing yoga exercises while listening to soft relaxing music.

The last she remembered, she saw the numbers on the clock roll over to one thirty. It was nine o'clock now. Did she really sleep almost eight hours? Was it possible she slept all night without waking and without a terrible nightmare?

There was a knock on the door.

"Sophia, it's Eloise; are you awake?"

"Come in, Eloise."

"My goodness, sleepyhead; you must have been up half the night to sleep this long. Are you feeling all right?"

"I'm feeling fine." Sophia didn't want Eloise to know she hadn't taken her pill the night before. Maybe it was a fluke that she didn't have a nightmare. It would be her secret, for now.

*****

Samantha was determined to get back to her writing. If she was lucky, and her mystery caught on, she would need to follow it up quickly with another. So many ideas were swirling around in her head. She told Megan not to disturb her unless it was a matter of life or death.

"If my mother calls, tell her whatever she decides is fine with me. I'm locking my door to the outside world."

"What about Fletch?"

"I don't think he'll call, but if he does, let me know."

Samantha was deep into the fourth chapter of the mystery when she suddenly had a thought about the real murder that had taken place.

"Whoever killed Richard Delaney," she shouted to the empty room, "wouldn't have hired a hit-man if they were a sharpshooter themselves."

A worried Megan knocked on the door.

"Samantha is everything all right in there?"

"Everything's fine." She opened the door. "All this time, we suspected the person responsible for Richard's murder had hired someone to kill him. What if that person was skilled with guns?"

"That would make sense; do you know of anyone like that?"

"No, but I could find out if any of the suspects is a marksman."

Samantha's determination to make progress on her book had diminished. She knew there would be no going back until she investigated the shooting ability of the suspects in Richard's murder. She placed a call to Fletch.

"Hello, sweetheart; it's good to hear your voice. I thought you were in solitary confinement all day while you write."

"That was the plan, but I had a thought. What if Richard's shooting wasn't done by a professional, but by someone who knew him. I'd be surprised if any of our persons of interest are marksmen, but it might be worth checking out."

"You have a point. I'm afraid I've let that investigation fall behind with Robin gone. I didn't appreciate how much work she actually does around here."

"Why don't I help out? I was thinking of calling Sophia to let her know Tony Horton is dead. I could also find out if she knows her way around guns. I think Cindy Matthews and Wanda Anderson might be able to give me information too."

"I should tell you to stay home and write your book, but I trust your instincts. Just promise me you'll be careful. You might not know these women as well as you think you do."

*****

"Megan, were there any calls?"

"Yes, your mother called twice; she's such a nice lady. We had a lovely conversation. You don't have to call her back; the three of us settled her questions."

"The three of you?"

"Your mother, your future mother-in-law and me. I think I'd like being a wedding planner. Sophia Delaney called too; she'd like you to call her. Your agent called and he had good news about pre-sales of your book. He wants you to call him as soon as possible, but he says don't stop writing. Also, there was a call from someone named Patsy Burke; she was in your high school class and wants to talk to you when you come home to Ashville. When I offered to take her phone number, she said it had waited a long time and could wait a while longer."

"I can't imagine why Patsy Burke would be calling me. I guess I'll find out in a few weeks.

"I'll be going out for a couple of hours. I'm glad you and my mother are getting along so well. Just remind her that Fletch and I want a simple wedding. If Arnie calls back again, tell him I'm still writing."

"You want me to lie to Arnie?" Megan laughed.

"Of course," said Samantha

*****

Samantha called Sophia from her car. She was happy to hear from her and welcomed a visit.

"Samantha, I couldn't wait to tell you; I had the best night's sleep I've had in ages. I took your advice and didn't take a pill last night. I tried yoga and soft music and it worked. I slept like a baby and didn't have a nightmare."

"That's good to hear, I have some information that might help relieve another worry for you. I asked Fletch to check on the whereabouts of Tony Horton. He discovered that Tony was the victim of a drive-by shooting months ago. There's no way you could have met him to arrange for Richard's murder whether you were sleepwalking or not."

"Tony Horton is dead? I'm sorry to hear that, but what a relief. That means I didn't hire him to kill Richard. He's not the only bad guy I knew back then; maybe I had him mistaken for someone else."

"Sophia, stop trying to convince yourself that you're a murderer. Tell me, do you have a gun in the house?"

"No, Richard didn't like guns. Eloise thought he should have one for protection, but he refused to even discuss it with her.

"I have another bit of good news," said Sophia. "I feel guilty about being so cheerful while I'm still in the mourning period for Richard, but I think he'd be happy for me. The director of *The Music Man* called this morning. My understudy has filled in for me but he wants me back for the last performance because next month we'll be going to Utica for a two-week stint. He thinks it's just the beginning and we will be on tour for several months."

"Sophia, that's wonderful. I'm so happy for you."

"If all goes as planned," she said, crossing her fingers, "I won't be in Lancashire for most of the year. I'd been thinking of putting the house on the market, and now I'm convinced it's a good idea. I still have my cabin in the woods and I like it there better."

"What about Eloise? Where will she go?"

"Oh, she doesn't live here; she has a place in town. She's been staying here at night to keep me company. I'm grateful to her, but I must admit, she's getting on my nerves."

"She does seem a little bossy," Samantha laughed.

"A little bossy? She's like a mother hen. Richard liked the attention at first, but I think he got tired of being treated like a child. Eloise doesn't know this, but he was talking to other people about managing his campaign for governor. I'm glad she never found out about his plans. She would have been crushed."

*****

Samantha had a good feeling that Sophia was going to be all right. She was hopeful the pills were a thing of the past. Maybe they weren't the cause of all Sophia's problems, but they certainly didn't help.

Samantha's next stop was to Cindy Williams' apartment. Cindy had just gotten off the phone with her former employer at the college. He was eager to have her return to the university. He'd tried three times to replace her and wasn't satisfied with any of the substitutes.

"Samantha, please come in."

"You're smiling, Cindy; something has made you very happy."

"Yes, I have my old job back at the university. Mr. Webster told me he didn't realize how valuable I was until he tried to replace me. Not only that, he's raising my salary. I'm beginning to feel good about life again."

Cindy offered her visitor a cup of tea. Samantha sat on the comfortable sofa in the living room.

"I really do love this apartment, and what you've done with it. Do you feel safe in the neighborhood?"

"Oh yes; it's close to the university and that can be a problem with some of the more rambunctious students, but I haven't had any trouble since the incident two years ago."

"What happened two years ago? Do you mind if I ask?"

"It wasn't serious. A young man who was helping in the mayor's office and attending the university, took a liking to me. At first, it was flattering, but it got out of hand when he followed me home one day and began showing up at my door for several weeks after that. My father insisted I have a gun for protection. He gave me a small handgun to keep in my nightstand.

"I took gun safety lessons, but I've never had to use the lessons or the gun."

"I take it you're not an expert shot."

"Oh, heavens no. I hate the thing. Don't tell my dad. I took the bullets out of the gun. I feel safer without them in there. Dad doesn't know, but I'd never have the nerve to pull the trigger on a real person."

"What happened with your stalker?"

"The police had a nice long talk with him. After that, his father pulled him out of school and took him back to Kansas. I don't think he was harmful, but I was relieved when he was gone."

"I don't blame you," said Samantha. "It could have ended badly."

Samantha believed Cindy didn't know enough about guns to fire the shot that had killed her former boss. She wished Cindy luck with her new old job. The women made plans to meet for lunch soon.

*****

Her next stop was to Mayor Wakefield's office where Margaret Wakefield was issuing orders to a professional decorator. There was something intimidating about the woman and Samantha was annoyed with herself that she felt uncomfortable around her.

"Hello, Mrs. Wakefield."

"Hello, Ms. Degan. What are you doing here? Did you have an appointment with the mayor?"

"No, ma'am. I stopped by to speak with Wanda Anderson, if she's not busy."

"That woman is busy being a meddler. She thinks she knows more about my husband's tastes than I do. I don't know why Forrest insists on keeping her on. She has gone to fetch me a sandwich from that inferior deli across the street. What in heaven's name could you want from her?"

"Nothing special," Samantha lied. "Maybe I'll come back some other time."

"No, I want you to get her out of my hair. She keeps watching me and André in our efforts to make this office worthy of the mayor of Lancashire."

Samantha noticed the look on André's face as he rolled his eyes. It was obvious he wasn't enjoying Mrs. Wakefield's company.

"Here's the little troll now," Margaret said loud enough for Wanda to hear.

Wanda grimaced as she set the sandwich down on a table by the wall.

"I hope this will be to your liking, Mrs. Wakefield. I asked them to make it just as you requested with white meat turkey only, extra thin slices of fresh tomato on cracked wheat bread."

"You imbecile! I asked for a whole wheat roll Can't you even handle a simple task? Ms. Degan is here to see you; take your lunch break now and get out of my sight."

Wanda walked out of the room with her shoulders slumped even further downward than normal.

"Wanda, I'm so sorry she spoke to you that way. Does Mayor Wakefield know how his wife treats you?"

"She's never rude when he's around. I tried to tell him what she's like, but I think he's afraid of her as much as the rest of us. She was never a very nice person, but being the first lady has made her a monster."

"Why do you put up with that treatment? I don't think I could tolerate working here if I were you."

"I'm hoping when the redecorating is finished, she won't be around as much. Not only that, I've worked for Mayor Wakefield for years. He's a wonderful man. I won't kid myself; no one wants to hire a plump, middle-aged woman even with my excellent clerical skills. Look around, you see nothing but young attractive people."

Samantha didn't agree that the world was like that outside of the mayor's office. She had to admit, most of the young women she observed were very attractive. Maybe they were left over from Richard Delaney's administration.

"What did you want to see me about, Samantha? I'm happy for the distraction, but did you want something specific?"

"You were so helpful the last time we talked. Since then, I've had a few nice visits with Cindy Matthews."

"Yes, Cindy Matthews, the one who shot her boss."

"I don't believe she did, Wanda; she admits to having feelings for him, but she didn't kill him or have him killed."

"Are you sure? I can see where someone might be tempted to commit murder."

"You aren't talking about Richard Delaney now, are you?"

"All I'm saying is that anyone who knocked off the illustrious First Lady of Lancashire would be a hero. I'm sorry, Samantha. I shouldn't even joke about murder."

"I don't blame you for feeling that way; there's no excuse for the way you were treated today. Poor André looked like he wanted to be anywhere but with Margaret Wakefield.

"I don't know how to ask you this, Wanda, other than to just say it. Do you know if either of the Wakefield's own guns?"

"Mayor Wakefield does some hunting. You're not suggesting Forrest killed Richard?"

"I'm not suggesting anything, but the fact remains that someone did kill him. Isn't it better to eliminate your boss from the list of suspects if he's innocent?"

"I guess so; he and Mrs. Wakefield were having dinner with friends when Richard was killed."

"I understand they were dining at Chung Lee's, only a few blocks from the theater. Maybe Mrs. Wakefield excused herself to go to the ladies' room, slipped out the door, shot the mayor and returned to their table as if nothing had happened."

"Oh, how I wish that were the truth. I can picture her sitting in a cold jail cell. It would serve her right, but I don't buy it. I doubt she owns a gun, and if she did, she'd probably never fire it herself. Mrs. Wakefield is well-known for hiring people to do everything for her."

"Maybe she hired a professional."

"It's possible, but I don't think she would. It was not a well-kept secret that Richard intended to throw his hat in the ring for the race for governor. He made it clear to Mayor Wakefield that he would be going it alone. I think that decision made Mrs. Wakefield happy because she didn't want her husband to be second banana state-wide as he was in the city. Forrest confided in me that his wife was happy that an upcoming election would force Richard to resign as mayor and Forrest would take over. Her goal was to be the first lady of Lancashire."

"What about Mayor Wakefield? Was he upset that Richard didn't ask him to run for lieutenant governor?"

"Forrest liked what he was doing before he became involved in politics. Don't get me wrong; he's a good leader. He doesn't have the looks Richard had, but he does have the brains to run the city. I know Richard couldn't have done it without Forrest. The only reason he took over as mayor was to please Margaret. That woman controls everything the poor man does."

"From what I've seen of Forrest Wakefield, he doesn't seem to be a murderer."

"That leaves me," smiled Wanda. "I can only tell you that I don't own a gun and I didn't hire someone to do the deed. I didn't have dreams of becoming executive assistant to the mayor. I'd prefer to be back in that accounting office on Cyprus Road. There was nothing more exciting than tax time. I miss the good old days."

"Thank you for being so honest with me. I knew you would be helpful. In the last few days, I've eliminated everyone on my list of suspects. I think it's easier to write a mystery than to solve one."

"Get that handsome detective friend of yours to help. I see you have a ring on your finger; does that mean you snagged the hunk? Don't look so surprised. Just because I'm gray haired and dowdy, doesn't mean I can't enjoy a pretty face."

"I'll be sure to tell Fletch you think he's pretty. I'm sure he'll be happy to hear it."

*****

This has been an interesting day, Samantha thought to herself. *I'm missing something, but what?*

CHAPTER 18

Samantha arrived at her apartment parking garage just as Fletch pulled into a vacant spot on the side street. They walked into the elevator together.

"How's my favorite sleuth tonight?" he said as he squeezed her hand. He wanted to pull her into his arms, but Mrs. Barkley and her three children were standing beside them. Molly, the youngest, stared at Fletch. She was holding a red, very sticky lollipop very close to the hem of his jacket.

The doors opened and the kids and Mrs. Barkley exited just in time to save Fletch a trip to the dry cleaner.

"I had a good day if you call eliminating suspects good. I'm stumped. I wish I was writing this mystery so I could drop a clue in the middle of the page."

Fletch listened when she told him about her conversations earlier in the day.

"I know how frustrating it can be but eliminating suspects is the way to go. Let's assume the killer is a sharpshooter. To keep up my skills, I don't go out in the streets and fire off my gun."

"You go to the shooting range; why didn't I think of that? If a person is an expert, they'd go to the shooting range regularly. I wonder how many shooting ranges are in the city?"

"We don't get many at the academy, although there are a few civilians who want to learn how to shoot a gun after they've bought one. We can check that out but this person has probably been shooting most of their lives."

"What are we looking for? I don't even have a name to check," lamented Samantha.

"Most reputable ranges have a sign-in. We start looking for any name that sounds familiar. I'll go with you tomorrow morning. I'd like to forget about murder tonight and concentrate on you."

They prepared dinner together. Samantha had to admit Fletch's cooking skills were much better than hers.

"I've lived on my own for longer than you. I had a choice of learning to cook or starving to death. Luckily, I found cooking relaxed me after a day with the bad guys."

They were enjoying the last bite of dinner when Samantha's computer made a sound indicating she had a call.

She turned it on and saw her mother and future mother-in-law together on the screen.

"Hello, darling; isn't this wonderful? Dennis came over and fixed me up so I can talk to you and see you at the same time."

"I'm glad he did that for you. Hello, Mrs. Fletcher."

"Hello, Samantha, dear; call me Sandy, please. Where's that handsome son of mine?"

"I'm right here, Mom; hello, Colleen."

"Hello, Fletch. Isn't this fun? You both look so well. I think it's because they're happy, don't you, Sandy?"

"Yes, they do have a glow about them. We called to go over wedding plans with you. Samantha, your mother and I wondered if you've gotten your dress yet?"

"I'll check my closet, but I'm sure I'll find one suitable for an outside wedding."

"Nonsense, Samantha. You'll need to buy something new. After all, you're only getting married one time. Don't you think your groom should see you in a pretty new frock?"

"Or without it," Fletch whispered in her ear.

"I heard that, son; you behave yourself."

"Yes, Mother."

"Mom, I told you, Fletch and I want a simple ceremony. Don't make us sorry we involved the two of you."

"Please go out and buy a new dress. I'll send you the money if you're worried about the cost."

"Mother, I think I can afford to pay for my wedding dress."

"Calm down; I know you're a grown-up, but you'll always be my baby."

"Okay, Mom, you win. I'll go shopping tomorrow. How are Dad and Jack?"

"They're doing great; they're out buying a new charcoal grill. Jack talked your dad into it. Those two men are getting along famously. You'd better not change your mind about marrying each other. The Fletchers are our new best friends.

"By the way, an old friend from high school, Patsy Burke called the other day. She asked for your phone number. I gave it to her; I hope that was all right."

"Yes, it's fine. I'll see what she wanted when I'm in Ashville."

"Probably just to wish you well, dear. You two have a wonderful evening and don't forget to go shopping tomorrow."

"Who's Patsy Burke?"

"I knew her in high school; we weren't especially close. I can't imagine why she's calling me. Maybe she's on the alumni committee and is making plans for our tenth reunion."

"I guess you'll be out shopping tomorrow."

"Not on your life, we have shooting ranges to visit."

"We can do that in the afternoon; I have some paperwork I should finish in the morning."

"I'll have Megan help me get a dress; she always looks nice. I was tempted to ask Mom to buy something for me, but I'm afraid it would be a fancy bridal gown. You don't mind that I want something simple, do you?"

"Whatever you choose will be fine with me. You look terrific in a pair of jeans and a t-shirt. I don't suppose your mom would go for that?"

She laughed as he slapped her gently on her jean covered behind.

CHAPTER 19

Megan arrived at the apartment, ready to work, at the usual hour.

"Don't even turn on your computer; I have another assignment for you."

"It sounds serious."

"It is serious and something I'm not looking forward to. I'd love it if you could go with me to look for a wedding dress. In fact, I'd love it if you would check out the bridesmaid dresses too. My mother tells me a maid of honor is required and I hope you'll agree to be mine."

"Samantha, I'm honored, but there must be others you've known longer than we've known each other."

"If knowing someone a long time is a prerequisite, I have no business marrying the groom. I don't have many friends, Megan, and I feel close to you. What do you say?"

"I would love to be your maid of honor, Samantha, that is, if my boss will let me have the day off."

"Your boss will let you have the week off since she will be on her honeymoon."

*****

Samantha dreaded entering the bridal shop Megan had suggested. She didn't want to try on a slew of fancy dresses. If only she and Fletch had run off to Las Vegas as he'd suggested. It was too late now; she was stuck.

As feared, a saleslady approached them even before the door to the shop closed behind them. She had a huge smile on her face showing off her shiny white teeth that seemed to sparkle as she spoke.

"I'm Miss Evelyn. Which of you lovely ladies is our bride?" she gushed.

"That would be Samantha," answered Megan.

"Samantha, what a beautiful name for a beautiful bride-to-be. Tell me, dear, when is our special day?" she said while scrutinizing her body.

"The wedding is in two weeks; it will in a chapel in the woods in Ashville. I want something very simple."

Samantha looked around the room and saw nothing but pure white dresses with miles of fabric and sparkling baubles even brighter than Miss Evelyn's teeth.

"Two-weeks?" Miss Evelyn cried, glancing at Samantha's belly. "I will need at least two months to special order the perfect gown. We will need several fittings before we're able to send you off to the most glorious day of your life."

"I understand; thank you for your time." Samantha turned to walk out the door when Miss Evelyn called her back.

"Now, wait just a moment. I might have a few dresses in the back. We can't guarantee perfection with so little time, but let me show you our choices."

"Remember, I want simple. Please don't bring out anything like those," she said, pointing at the window display.

Miss Evelyn's smile faded, but a sale was a sale. She disappeared into the next room.

"I don't think Miss Evelyn is happy."

"Miss Evelyn's happiness is not my concern. Will you look at the prices on these things? Some of them cost more than a new car."

Miss Evelyn walked back into the sales area rolling a rack filled with dresses. At first glance, Samantha could tell they were not as outlandish as the ones she'd already seen.

Instead of letting her look through the rack herself, Miss Evelyn held each dress up individually. The woman made Samantha nervous and she wished she'd walked out of the shop when she had the chance.

She finally spotted one she liked—an off-white full length, form-fitting A-line satin gown. Megan nodded in approval and Samantha walked toward the dressing room with Miss Evelyn following.

She resisted the temptation to tell the overly attentive saleslady to back off.

Samantha came out of the dressing room.

Megan's eyes grew wide. "Samantha, you look beautiful; the one shoulder style looks so sexy. Fletch is going to freak out when he sees you."

"I hope he doesn't do that, but do you really think it looks okay? It's not as simple as I wanted, but I do love the dress."

"You look lovely, my dear," Miss Evelyn chimed in. "Your height and slimness are perfect for this style. I wish all my brides had a figure like yours. Let us find a suitable veil for you."

"I won't need a veil, but you could direct Megan to the bridesmaids' dresses."

*****

Twenty minutes later, they walked out of the bridal shop, each carrying their dresses. The realization that she and Fletch were going to be married in two short weeks hit Samantha and she was beginning to feel like a bride-to-be.

Fletch was waiting for her when she returned to her apartment.

"Close your eyes," Samantha said when he opened the door.

"I can't see anything; it's covered with a garment bag."

"I don't care; just close your eyes."

Samantha carefully hung her dress in the closet and returned to the living room to greet him properly.

"Oh, Fletch, it's finally sinking in that we're going to be husband and wife in a matter of days."

"You're not changing your mind, are you?"

"And miss wearing the fabulous dress I just bought?"

"I took your suggestion and asked Mike to be my best man. He said yes, but it probably had more to do with Megan being your maid of honor than with his friendship with me."

*****

On the way to one of the largest shooting ranges in town, Samantha told him about Miss Evelyn and her bridal shop experience.

"Megan apologized all the way home for suggesting we go there. It turned out fine and gives us something we'll have fun laughing about when we've had a bad day."

Fletch pulled into the parking lot of the shooting range.

Samantha felt nervous about going inside the large facility. She'd never been to a shooting range before and didn't know what to expect.

The young man at the check-in desk was far from the intimidating Neanderthal type she'd pictured. He seemed to be in his early twenties with a boyish look that would probably be with him until middle age.

"Good afternoon," he said, watching Samantha. "This must be your first time at a shooting range."

"How did you guess?"

"You'd be surprised how many people have a look of panic on their faces when they walk through those doors for the first time."

"Pal, we aren't here for target practice. I'm Detective Fletcher from the Lancashire Police Department." Fletch held out his badge. "This is Samantha Degan; we're investigating a recent crime and would like to look at your registration log."

Suddenly, the friendly young man's shoulders stiffened and the boyish smile left his face.

"You got a search warrant?"

"I can get one but you could make my life easier if you would just let me look at the log."

Fletch felt Samantha's hand on his arm.

"Look who's walking out of the restroom."

Fletch turned his head to the left.

"Well, I'll be darned. I do believe we've found our murderer," he whispered quietly enough that the desk clerk couldn't hear him.

"Is it all right if we watch from the windows out here. As you guessed, I've never been to a shooting range before."

"I guess it'll be okay; just be quick about it. People get nervous around cops."

They stepped up to the observation window and watched as their suspect gripped a handgun like an expert and hit the target each time a shot was fired.

"I'm hungry," said Fletch as they pulled away from the shooting range parking lot.

"How can you be hungry? We just watched a cold-blooded murderer showing no mercy at that poor defenseless target."

"That was some fine shooting. Richard Delaney was definitely the target that night and he didn't stand a chance."

"What are you going to do?"

"First, I'm going to fortify myself with a cheeseburger, and then we'll pay a visit to Ms. Eloise Kittredge."

"What if she doesn't go home from the shooting range?"

"Then we wait until she's home."

"Now that you mention it, I'm a tad hungry myself. A cheeseburger does sound tempting, although I should be eating salads all week. I can't gain an ounce of weight or I won't fit into my wedding dress," she sighed.

*****

While they were enjoying their cheeseburgers and greasy fries, Samantha wondered aloud what prompted Eloise to kill Richard.

"If she's cooperative, we'll find out today. I suspect he was no longer in need of her services. Maybe he was preparing for the governorship with a whole new cast of characters. Richard Delaney didn't strike me as the most loyal guy in town."

CHAPTER 20

Fletch and Samantha waited in the car for less than thirty minutes before Eloise Kittredge pulled into the driveway of her modest home.

"Hello, Detective Fletcher. I've been expecting you. Won't you both come in? I'll make us some tea."

Samantha noted the calmness in her voice as they walked to the front door and Eloise invited them inside.

"Please have a seat; you don't mind if I make a pot of tea, I hope. I'd prefer a brandy, but I think I'd better opt for the tea."

The room was pleasant, despite the old-fashioned furniture and dated curtains. There were photographs lining the fireplace mantle. Richard was in every one of them: Richard with the governor, Richard being sworn in as mayor, and Richard standing with several of the prominent people of Lancashire.

"Doesn't Eloise have any family?" she whispered, not knowing Eloise was walking in with a tray of tea and cookies at that moment.

"Richard and Sophia are my family. I was an only child; my father died the day after I graduated from college. Mother was sickly ever since giving birth to me and was unable to care for herself. After Father's death, she became an invalid and completely dependent on me, her caregiver. I suppose it was only right that she robbed me of a normal life because I'd robbed her of her health when I was born.

"Mother passed away five years ago. After caring for her all those years, I was suddenly alone in the world. I hadn't held a job or had any type of social life because of my duties to Mother.

"For all those years, I didn't leave the house except to push Mother's wheelchair to the corner and back every day, weather permitting. The supermarket filled our order once a week and any clothing we needed was all done through mail order. I had plenty of time to watch the cable news stations daily and became interested in politics.

"Shortly after Mother's passing, I read about Richard Delaney considering a mayoral run. I went out to the department store and bought myself a new wardrobe. I went to a beauty shop for the first time in almost forty years and had my hair styled and my nails done. Richard was still working out of his law office then and I marched in there and announced that I would be his campaign manager.

"Of course, I didn't know the first thing about running a campaign, but I read everything I could get my hands on. I talked to the staff in the governor's office and our senator's office, and learned what I could. Poor Richard didn't know any more than I did and he thought I knew exactly what I was doing. Something must have worked. He won the election in a landslide.

"Richard and Sophia became the children I'd never had, I don't know what Sophia will do without Richard and me when I'm sent to prison. Samantha, I know you have begun a friendship with the dear girl; will you watch out for her?"

"Of course, I will, Eloise. You don't have to worry about Sophia; she's a strong woman and will do fine."

"Richard was true to her, you know. Most people thought he was a womanizer. It's true, he had an eye for women, especially blondes. He was like a kid in a candy shop; he loved looking at the options, but he always chose his favorite, and that was Sophia.

"He was a prince, all right," Fletch said as he felt Samantha's elbow in his side. "What can you tell us about the night Richard died?"

"I didn't mean to kill him. I know it looks like I planned it, but I didn't.

"You see, Father always wanted a boy to go hunting with. He took me when I was about five and I was a mess. I hated firing a gun and I cried when I watched him kill a beautiful fawn. He was ashamed of my behavior and insisted on teaching me how to shoot and how to kill. As I grew older, I went to the shooting range with him and learned to respect guns as I learned to hit my target. I didn't do much shooting for years until after Mother died. I began going back to the shooting range. I found it calmed me after a long, hard day. I never went hunting again because I found shooting animals abhorrent.

"The night of Sophia's performance, I decided to stay behind because I wanted to work on re-writing the speech Richard would be giving the following day. Just before Richard left the office, he told me he wouldn't need me as his campaign manager when he ran for governor. Just like that, he dismissed me as though I was nothing but a paid employee.

"I was in a terrible state. I couldn't breathe. What would I do for the rest of my life and what would I do without Richard and Sophia to care for? Sophia needed me and Richard was taking her away. They would move to the governor's mansion and I would be all alone.

"I don't know how long I sat in that lonely office, but I remember driving home in a daze.

"I keep many types of guns here in my home. I unlocked the cabinet and took out my favorite pistol and a silencer that I purchased so I could practice at outdoor shooting ranges without those heavy ear protectors.

"I drove to the theater and parked in the lot behind the building that's reserved for actors and crew. I knew the side door would be unlocked. I'd seen many run through performances and dress rehearsals to know at what point the cast would be parading up and down the aisles. I waited until the music was at its loudest and opened the door. Everyone was looking at the middle aisle as I pointed my gun at Richard's head and pulled the trigger. I turned and walked out just the way I came in. I could still hear the music faintly as I pulled out of the parking lot and drove home."

"I hope you know, I would never have let anyone go to prison for Richard's murder. I think I always knew the crime would be solved eventually. I'm ready to go, Detective. No hard feelings. I realize you're just doing your job.

Eloise Kittredge walked out of the home she'd known for all her life without a glance backward.

CHAPTER 21

"There's another crime you solved, Samantha; you're pretty good at this."

"I didn't really solve it, Fletch, I'd say it solved itself."

"You're the one who spotted Eloise Kittredge when we were at the shooting range. I was too busy arguing with that punk kid."

"It was only a matter of time before Eloise confessed. She looked like a load had been lifted off her shoulders when she was spilling the beans about the shooting. I feel sorry for her, Fletch, but her relationship with Sophia and Richard wasn't a healthy one."

"I don't often feel sorry for cold-blooded killers," said Fletch. "Eloise had a pretty sad life. She had no life of her own. All she did for almost forty years was sit in the house with her mother. I'm going to stop complaining about our mothers and their plans for our wedding. We're lucky to have them."

"Do you think Eloise's birth really caused her mother's health problems?"

"She might have had a stroke or a neurological problem, but I suspect it was a bad case of hypochondria. What a wasted life for both."

*****

They arrived at Samantha's apartment.

"What would you like to do tonight, Fletch?"

"I wouldn't mind kicking back on your sofa and watching television; how about you?"

"That sounds heavenly. I wonder if I should call Sophia to let her know about Eloise. She might need some TLC tonight."

"You're probably right; why don't you give her a call to see if she's home? We can go right over."

Samantha punched in her number. Sophia answered on the first ring.

"Samantha, I was just about to call you and ask if you'd be able to come over to my place."

"You must have heard about Eloise."

"What about Eloise? Is she all right? I haven't been able to reach her."

"I'll be there in ten minutes."

"Tell me, Samantha, what has happened to Eloise?"

"I'm sorry, Sophia. Eloise confessed to murdering Richard."

"Murdering Richard? That can't be; there must be some mistake. Eloise loved Richard like a son."

"I'm afraid it's true. Did you know Eloise is a sharp shooter? Richard told her he was going to replace her and it sounds like she snapped."

"Richard was an idiot. I'm sorry to speak of him like that but he wasn't a very nice person. I loved him, but I was never blind to his faults. Poor Eloise; she must be miserable."

"Actually, I think she's relieved to have it out in the open. She had a very sad life before she met you."

"I know she was a caregiver for her mother. I always wondered if she had a life outside of that dreary little house. I'll do anything I can to help her but not tonight. Will you stop by?"

"We're on our way."

*****

Except for an outside light on the front porch, the large house looked to be completely dark.

"Oh, dear," said Samantha. "Sophia seemed calm on the phone. I wonder if the shock has set in."

The door opened. Sophia was smiling. "Come into the living room."

"What happened to the lights? Why is it so dark in here?"

With that, the lights flashed on and Samantha heard *Surprise* being shouted from the room.

Megan was there along with Robin, Cindy Matthews, and Wanda Anderson. Her old friends Amy Griffin and Daphne Morgan and the ladies from Stonehill Manor all gathered around her, hugging her and smiling from ear to ear.

There were balloons hanging from the ceiling, crepe paper streamers around the windows and fireplace. Brightly wrapped packages and champagne that had obviously been flowing for a while.

Frank Wells and Mike each grabbed Fletch by an arm.

"You're coming with us, buddy. We'll let the ladies have their champagne; this is a night for beer and brats. Half the department is waiting for you at Marge's Saloon."

"Have fun!" Fletch shouted as he was being escorted out the door.

"You too," Samantha said, blowing him a kiss. She couldn't help but wonder what Eloise was doing at that very moment.

Sophia pulled her aside. "I'm worried about Eloise, but she's a strong lady. She would want us to have a good time. I'll go there tomorrow to see what I can do."

Samantha sipped her champagne and felt every inch a bride-to-be surrounded by her friends.

EPILOGUE

Instead of counting weeks until the wedding, Samantha was counting days.

In six days, she would be Mrs. Joseph Fletcher. She would keep Samantha Degan as her professional name but she was anxious to be officially known as Mrs. Samantha Fletcher. Mrs. Fletcher had a familiar ring to it. Could it have been from an old television show her parents liked to watch? She didn't care; it would be her name now and she would keep it forever.

"I'm starting to get butterflies," Megan told her when she arrived for work that morning. I've never been a maid of honor before; I hope I don't do anything stupid."

"What stupid thing could you do?"

"Well, I could blubber all over the place. I'm just so happy for you and Fletch. You see what I mean," she said as the tears streamed down her cheeks.

"You'll do fine; you'll be cried out by next Saturday."

*****

"Have you heard from Sophia today?"

"Yes, she called earlier. The lawyer wanted to arrange bail for Eloise, but she wouldn't allow it. Sophia said Eloise seems perfectly happy sitting in a jail cell until her trial. She's made friends with a woman who was arrested for attempted robbery along with her no-good boyfriend. I'm sure she's being a mother hen to her. Sophia thinks she will plead guilty to killing Richard. She says she is guilty so why would she say she isn't? It's such a sad story."

"Sophia will be riding with Mike and me to the wedding. She seems like a different person since she stopped taking that supplement."

"Those pills did cause a reaction. I'm happy she could give them up. Her therapist has been helpful too. It's good for Sophia to talk about her feelings. I think she'll be just fine."

"Cindy Matthews has offered to drive Wanda to Ashville. Believe it or not, I think Wanda has gotten over her resentment of Cindy. I'm glad you invited them both."

"To be honest, I didn't think about inviting them, but when I saw them at my shower, it seemed the right thing to do, I don't want to leave anyone out. Even the gang from Stonehill Manor will be coming. It was so good to see everyone. I don't get out there as often as I'd like.

"I'd better get to work. I left my heroine dangling from a drawbridge. If I don't get her to safety, I'll worry about her during our entire honeymoon."

*****

The storyline was going smoothly when Samantha's cell phone sounded and startled her. She answered without checking to see the identity of the caller.

"Hello."

"Is this Samantha Degan?" asked the woman caller.

"Yes, it is. How may I help you?"

"Samantha, my name is Patsy Burke. I don't know if you remember me, I was a classmate in high school."

Samantha didn't let on that she barely remembered the name.

"Hello, Patsy, I'm sorry I missed you last week. You didn't leave a number, so I wasn't able to return the call."

"That's all right. I read in the local paper that you are going to be married in Ashville. I understand you solved a murder that took place in Lancashire."

"Oh my, I didn't solve the professor's murder single-handedly. There were many factors and many people involved in the case."

"I'm sure, but I don't know where to start, that's why I'm calling you."

"Suppose you tell me what this is all about, Patsy. I'll be glad to help if I can. Are you writing a mystery novel, by chance?"

"If only that were so. Do you remember Chandler Sinclair? Most of the kids called him C.J.; he was very popular."

"Of course, I remember C.J. He died in a fall while hiking. It was a horrible tragedy for his family as well as the school and the entire city."

"What if I told you I have evidence it wasn't an accident? What if I told you someone pushed him off that precipice?"

"Patsy, it happened several years ago. The police did a thorough investigation and determined it was an accidental fall. C.J. lost his footing and slipped off the cliff to his death. What evidence do you have?"

"I can't talk about it over the telephone. Is there any way you can meet me when you get to Ashville?"

"My mother has me on a tight schedule. I'll give you a call when I arrive and arrange to meet with you. Why don't you come to the wedding? The ceremony will be in the chapel at Wedgwood Park with a reception following at the Ashville Hilton.

"I'll wait for your call; I really need to talk to you..." The phone went dead.

From what Samantha remembered of Patsy Burke, she was a quiet girl. She didn't think of her as having a flair for the dramatic. *What possible evidence could she have that C.J. was murdered?*

*****

Samantha was carefully packing her suitcases for her trip to Ashville. She thought, by arriving early she could help with last minute details and visit with her old friends. She packed clothes for the Ashville visit and for their short honeymoon after the wedding. Fletch was stretching it to be away from work for too long during Robin's maternity leave. They would have a real vacation after her return.

"Your Mom's on the phone," Megan called out from the other room. "She sounds upset, I hope there isn't anything wrong."

"Hi, Mom; what's up?"

"Patsy Burke was seriously injured in an automobile accident."

She could hear Colleen Degan's words in her ear. *The police suspect foul play.*

THE END

ABOUT THE AUTHOR

 Jane O'Brien is a wife, mother of three, and grandmother of five. Jane and her husband, Dave, have lived in several states in their over fifty years of marriage. They are retired and live in Northern Colorado. Jane enjoys writing mysteries and family and friendship novels. *Murder in Stonehill Manor* is the first in the Samantha Degan Mystery series, followed by this book—*Murder in Lancashire*.

www.ingramcontent.com/pod-product-compliance
Lightning Source LLC
Chambersburg PA
CBHW020343260626
47156CB00004B/1671